Cry, Little Girl

Based On A True Story

Chelsea Nicole

To my Grandpa Frank and my Grandma Marjorie
for doing everything you possibly could to
gain custody of us. You never failed us.

PROLOGUE

I was eleven years old when my mother tried to kill us.

When I close my eyes and try to draw up the memory, it arrives disjointed and fleeting, like peering through a kaleidoscope at a feather drifting in the wind. The shapes are there; I can see them moving. But sometimes they are indistinguishable from one another. There is my mother, crying in the bathroom, her beautiful blonde hair tousled and wet as she weeps. Awful, gut-wrenching sobs echo off the tile walls. There is Tim, his eyes wide with intention, his big gnarled hands clenching and unclenching in anticipation—of what? My brother, Matthew, walks slow-motion down the hallway toward me, his face grim with unknowing. My sister—I glance around—where is she?

"Come on," Tim says to me, a shadow without a face. "We're going down to the river."

"Why?" I ask.

"Gonna play hide and seek."

"At the river?" Matthew asks.

"Why's Mom crying?" I demand, as he leads us to the back door.

"Enough with the questions."

The screen door, its wire mesh pinpricked with holes, creaks open and a gust of cool air ruffles my dress. Outside, the afternoon sun is obscured by a mass of grey clouds, all dark in their centers and swollen with rain. Raindrops peck at my hair, my face. Glancing upward, they peck my eyes and run down my cheeks like freshly fallen tears.

I can still hear the wracking sobs. They penetrate my heart. Each one is like a blow to the stomach, and then I hear, *"My babies!"*

Beneath my bare feet, the grass is slick with rain. My toes dig into the mud and make squishy sounds. "What's she saying?" I ask ponderously. The woods are drawing nearer. I can see the river through the trees.

Tim doesn't seem to hear me. And then the images go away, are replaced by the feeling of cold and wet and worry. Lightning cracks the sky but I'm not even sure lightning is really there. Looking around now, I'm not sure of anything. The images are vibrating, moving swiftly out of focus. Everything is awash with rain and the sobs are unbearable.

Tim grips my wrist and hurries me away from the house. Away from Mom.

In the distance, sirens.

Blue and red flashing lights.

Car doors opening, closing.

Police radios crackling.

Heavy boots on linoleum.

The screen door creaking open.

Tim lets go of my wrist. Matthew and I run back, back the

way we came. To the house. Everything is slow now, like a dream.

My mom. Mascara tears dripping down her face, her eyes wide and red and insane as she is ushered through the living room with her hands behind her back. The police officer holding her wrists is not gentle. “My babies!” she cries. Matthew and I stand perfectly still, watching. She looks at us one last time, but she doesn’t *see* us. Not really. Behind her eyes is a big mess. The cop has a hand on her head as she ducks down and climbs into the back of the police car. The rain is very heavy now. I can hardly see.

Tim comes next. Two police officers flanking him. He says nothing, and he does not look at us.

Then the police cars are driving away, and a thick blanket is wrapped around my bare shoulders. “Your aunt is on her way,” a reassuring voice says. “You’re all right now. You’re safe.”

“Where’s my mom going?”

“Shhh.

“But…”

“I like your dress,” the voice assures me. “What are those, sunflowers?”

Forgetting everything, I peer down at my dress.

“Yes,” I tell her.

Sunflowers.

CHAPTER 1

I grew up in a trailer in Newnan, Texas.

It was old and blue, its skirting all torn up. Mom was a pack rat, so stuck to every inch of the wall were random pictures and cheap, tacky décor. It was as if she'd gone through every thrift store, antique shop and junkyard in town to cobble together all the odds and ends that haunted our walls—a panoramic mosaic of unfitting pieces. She always went overboard with the decorations—nowadays I see it as the earliest glimpse I had into her scattered, overcrowded mind. A composite of her cracked psyche. A warning.

I didn't like many of the decorations, but there were flowers, too.

Unlike the rest of it, these pictures I enjoyed. These were images no faltering human vision could sully. They were my windows into places timeless and untouchable. They made me wonder about my mother. There were colorful daisies, lilies, tulips, and dandelions. All the beautiful flowers my mom loved but couldn't grow in the sun-baked Texan dirt outside our home. Of course, she could have enlisted one of her male friends to put together a makeshift raised bed, while another could have delivered the potting soil. Who knows? And if she really wanted to simplify things, she could have gone to Walmart for cheap planters and soil and flowers galore. But my mom wasn't into that sort of thing. Back then, she was too busy drinking. To nourish life to health would mean to step out into the bleary banks of non-drunkenness, an undertaking not meant for a perpetually drunk woman.

Regardless, I especially loved the kitchen, which had a sunflower theme. She did a nice job there. We even had yellow napkins on the kitchen table, which was covered by a plastic tablecloth with sunflower prints. I'd press my thumb upon the flat petals, leaving faint oil-trails of my fingerprints. My brother Matthew, three years older than me, would pretend to do his homework at the table while I sat watching him.

One afternoon, he looked at me with mild irritation. "*What*?" he asked.

I shrugged my shoulders. "Nothing."

"Why're you looking at me?"

Another shrug. "Dunno."

"Quit it," he growled.

"What're you drawing?" I asked.

Doodles and stick figures covered the page he was working on. He quickly covered it with his binder and scrunched his face up into a mean scowl. He leaned in close to my face. "None of your damn business."

"Hey! You can't say that!"

"The hell I can't."

I must have gasped at the double cursing. He was mean to me, and I felt like hurting him. "Mooooom!" I hollered.

Matthew's eyes went wide then. They always say that a mother loves all her children equally, but that wasn't the case with mine. She hated Matthew, ever since he was a little boy. He was an *accident*, she used to say. But also, I think maybe it's because she saw so much of my father in him, and she hated him, too. Guilty by proxy of DNA, or wicked chromosomes. Whatever the case, Mom put the fear of God in my brother.

"Shhhh!" Matthew quickly hushed me, eyes pleading. "Don't!"

But it was too late.

At the end of the hall, my mom's bedroom door lurched open and a nude man appeared in the doorway. Sweat glistened on his body, his arms and stomach rippled with muscle. All over, he was stained with grease, a disheveled Adonis. Locks of long black hair were matted to his forehead; he swept them back, revealing a pair of dark, angry eyes. "What do you kids want! Can't you see I'm busy?"

But that was the strange thing: I hadn't asked for this man —whatever his name was. I had asked for my mom.

"Where's Mom?" I demanded. At nearly six years old, I hadn't yet lost an ounce of confidence. These were *my* sunflowers surrounding his hot stinking flesh. These were the mirrors shoring thousands of *my* life's glances. Of *my* mother's. The world was brand new, and I felt uniquely capable of making it abide by my wishes, however great. My youthful vision was as big as the child's one-room planet, possible and endless.

Matthew, on the other hand, froze. Fish-hooked. Two dead-fin eyes, flat as a broken clock.

The muscular man frowned. "Busy," he said. "Go to your room. The both of you."

"Fine," I fired back.

I stood up and walked across the plush rugs covering every inch of floor, all the faces on the walls leering at me. Carnie distortions, indignant and disparate, flickered past. Matthew followed behind, and the man slammed the door. The hallway was covered with mirrors, making it seem like an army of our clones was marching past with exact precision. Reaching my bedroom on the right at the end of the hall, I sat on the bed and opened a picture book, riffling through the pages.

Our rooms were attached by a bathroom, and Mom's room was on the opposite side. Through her door I could hear the steady rhythmic crunching of bedsprings. The man was panting heavily, saying things I did not understand.

I flipped a page.

During that time, Newnan was rural with one main highway called 211, where the main businesses were. Old Town Newnan had meat markets and farmer's markets. The area where we lived was for low-income families, all of us blank-faced people baking beneath the same dull flag of poverty. We only lived there because of my father, Bob, who was a mechanic and had a shop a couple of miles down the road from our house.

Bob didn't live with us at the trailer, though. He stopped

by frequently, mostly to visit Matthew, but my grandparents disapproved of him because he went to jail a lot for abusing my mom. My mom was 26 when she had me, my dad 30. If they'd known what they were in for, I think they'd have done it all differently. But who knows?

A few hours later, after falling asleep with the book in my lap, I awoke to the sound of NASCAR blaring on the television. Static and other people's excitement foamed through my ears. There was a race going on, and the man was shouting in support of one of the drivers. The air was stale with cigarette smoke, which crept under my door and unfurled like slowly creeping mustard gas.

Wiping sleep from my face, I fumbled down the hallway, which was dark now. The mirrors cast shadowed reflections of me. In the living room was the man, but no Mom. She must have 'gone to the store.'

Dressed in whitewash jeans with no shirt, the man was sitting on the couch, drinking beer and smoking cigarettes. He was awash in adult agitation, pink-faced and twitching toward the television. Matthew was nowhere near. Probably too intimidated.

I liked the sound of the cars as they zipped around corners.

Warrrrunnnngggg.

Lost boomerangs and sonic circles. The sound of ghastly retreat, and return.

My eyes were plastered to the TV, mesmerized. There was a La-Z-Boy next to the couch; I sat on it without realizing, my eyes not lifting from the screen. Clearly this was an event of high anticipation, thunder and color kernelling constantly from scene to scene. The man stubbed out cigarette after cigarette on the stained metal coffee table between us. Cracked open another beer. “Come on, chickenshit! Catch up to him!”

After a while, the front door creaked open, and Mom came inside. She was a small lady with strawberry blonde hair. Very pretty. Big, beautiful eyes, floaty and crepuscular. A sideways, whimsical specter. She was wearing a yellow summer dress, and in her arms was a big paper bag. She set it down on the table alongside her keys and produced two six packs of beer and several cartons of cigarettes from the bag. She immediately handed one of the cartons to the man, saying, “Here ya go, babe.”

She called everyone that. The men, that is. I think mostly because she didn’t remember their names. How could she, when there were so many?

Not turning his head from the TV, the man accepted the cigarettes without ceremony, as if they were her penance for having done something wrong to him. But he was in our trailer, eating *our* food, drinking our beer and smoking our cigarettes. I wondered quite hard why he felt entitled to such good treatment. Was it his looks? His stature, or rugged anger?

What happened next, I’ll never forget. It was the first time in my life that I felt real pain.

The man, his eyes all glossy and unblinking, reached over to stub out his cigarette, but he missed. This time he reached a little too far. He plunged the cigarette into the flesh of my forearm. I cried out, snatching my arm, tears immediately filling my eyes. He was right there, smiling at me.

He had done it on purpose.

I looked up, searching frantically for my mother. Desperate to find her face and to see some comfort there—love, even. Desperate for the instinct of her protection, for the comfort of maternity.

Vacancy instead. Her silhouette shrouded, standing silent at the couch's end. Her pale eyes reflected my stare, offering nothing. Her gaze met the fresh meat of my cigarette-sized flesh, the black smell of it. She made no move toward my sorrow. I watched as she gazed right past it like a dumb chunk of melting ice. Mother was empty, all spilled out. She was somewhere I was not.

The shock wore off then, dropping like a sheet and leaving me cold. I sprang to my feet, all the pain and fear rushing in. I ran screaming down the hallway, clutching my arm against my body like a broken doll. I didn't know where I was headed—away from that man, and from that cold, empty figure of my mother, that was for sure.

I reached the end of the hallway and stood panting, feeling directionless. To my left, Matthew's bedroom door opened swiftly. We faced each other, him with his usual grimace, brow furrowed and mouth turned down. His hand lingered on the door. I assumed he would tell me to shut up, and probably kick or pinch me, too. He reached out for me, and I turned away, bracing.

Matthew grabbed the collar of my shirt and pulled me

into his room, closing the door behind us. He guided me by the shoulders and set me down on his bed, then he walked back and locked the door.

Click.

Looking back, I realize this was the first and only time Matthew was ever nice to me.

CHAPTER 2

My dad used to tell a lot of stories about his past that were difficult to prove, and the following was one of them.

In certain areas in Michigan back in the 1960s, kids were allowed to drive their parents around in the family vehicle. On a particularly wet and cold winter's day, my uncle Carl was doing just that—driving his mother to the local grocery store—when he hit a patch of black ice, lost control of the vehicle, and flipped it upside down into an embankment on the edge of some farmland. My grandmother, not wearing a seatbelt, was ejected through the windshield and crashed into the barbwire fence along the perimeter of the farm. She died there, tangled in the barbed wire, long before the paramedics arrived. Once my grandfather learned the news, he went home and immediately hung himself. He preferred to kill himself than to sleep beside her bedside cavity. In my family, the fear of aloneness is a hereditary sickness.

My dad and his brother and sisters became orphans overnight. In order to survive, they were forced to drop out of school and work on a farm to make ends meet. I was never able to verify this story—I tried getting in touch with my father's sister, Eleanor, but she died suddenly before we could speak. Silence at its fatal speed. My dad didn't attend her funeral.

If this story were true, it might help explain many of

the things I experienced growing up. In a matter of moments, a whole family was utterly destroyed. One more microscopic empire to be plundered by the cumbersome clock-hand. Those that were left went on to live hard lives rife with poverty and abuse, and the abuse crossed generations, a slow and soundless destruction. A cherry-cloud in the eye of a fresh-born baby.

I often wonder about the past. What might my life have been like had my father's parents survived—if in fact they were killed in a car crash as my dad has claimed? He wouldn't have had to drop out of school. His education likely would have gone past that of the fifth grade; he might have even attended college, gotten a degree, and pursued a respectable career. There could have been self-actualization above the soil and soot of circumstance. Instead of working as a mechanic in a greasy old shop with few patrons—drinking Milwaukee beer throughout the day while tinkering with this and that—he could have been a doctor. A teacher. An engineer. A Somebody on the lucky side of life, unscorned by the curse of tragedy.

Then, I wonder: would he still have fallen in love with my mother: the carefree, wild, beautiful woman who was never afraid to speak her mind? Would their fates still have so meticulously aligned? Would the sum still be the same? I'd like to think so. And maybe then we'd have grown up in a loving household, and all those things that happened would be just as this is—a fantasy. Unreal. Intangible.

My mom, in stark contrast, grew up in a loving home with married parents who doted on her, which is why I find it hard to believe we're a product of our parents. To me that seems a cheap excuse to be a bad person without accepting blame for one's actions. Or else an inevitable proof that moral abandon is self-chosen, self-conscious. Somewhere the gravid love of her parents got lost in translation—either in birth or in life. At some point that tender history was evacuated from my mother's gaze, leaving only ghosts, and their bones.

To my knowledge, Mom never saw her parents having sex in the living room with their children around, and yet she would do this constantly while we were growing up. Perhaps it was some hitch in the genetic link. I first witnessed it at four years old, when, to my horror, I heard loud moans and screams echoing down the hallway as I was playing with my toys. I immediately became scared, but even so I rushed into the living room, where I saw Mom completely naked having sex with a man. It was a ritual unknowable and obscene. The present, piercing animal sounds of my mother displaced every lullaby she might have cooed to me.

Not knowing what it meant, I raced back to Matthew's room and pushed the door open.

"Why is Mom wrestling with a boy? Or hugging?" I demanded, perplexed.

He was lying on his bed reading a motorsports magazine. He looked up, unfazed as a retired prophet. "Well *duh*. They're having sex, idiot," he said, then got up and closed the door in my face. No more enlightenment for today.

It was around this time that my mother started going on long sex and drinking benders. Several men would come home with her at night while drunk and have sex with her

—oftentimes in the living room while Matthew and I were watching TV, which forced us to get up and retreat to our rooms while the trailer thumped and shook. We quickly became the vestiges of energy expended and reinvested elsewhere. Peripheral. Flowers in the attic.

Then the men would disappear, interspersed with visits from my dad, who would stay for days or weeks at a time, drinking long into the night with Mom and fighting. A spinning saloon door of resentment, festered and unleashed. Sometimes I'd hear them screaming at each other, and on more than one occasion my dad resorted to physical violence, beating Mom bloody until she stopped arguing or stopped moving altogether. Usually she would take it, but every so often she would get pissed off and call the police. The last time she did that, he went to jail for a couple of years.

I only visited him once during this time: not that I had any choice in the matter either way. I didn't actively avoid him; Mom just never took me. Her blank stoicism made it hard to guess her intentions. I've always wondered if somehow the satisfaction of seeing her abuser behind bars couldn't compensate for the wounds of his absence. The one time I did visit, I strolled down the cells singing the theme song to Cops: *"Bad boys, bad boys, whatcha gonna do? Whatcha gonna do when they come for you?"*

I don't think I was trying to be an asshole—it just seemed appropriate. I remember some of the inmates chuckling. Others were visibly angered, which made me sing louder. They couldn't get me, after all. I could taunt them from the other side of the bars—the good side—and they could try all they wanted to squeeze their big fat arms through and give me what I deserved. And I could just laugh and laugh, a skinny little girl with all the power. I didn't realize then my source of power was my simple naivety. The power of youth lies in its ease at slicing the world into digestible separation. When you're young, picking sides is easy. It was as clear-cut as the oxidized bars of steel framing out my father's face.

My dad banned me from visitation after that, most likely because he got his ass kicked by those angry inmates. He was never a physically strong person, which is probably why he only chose to hurt people smaller than him: children and women. His power lay at the opposite end of mine. It came from the rank opportunism of a seasoned offender, decades of exploiting weakness. Quick to molder behind the contraption that slid shut with a bang.

When Mom told me this news, I was unmoved. Casually unpacking her beer and cigarettes (groceries were often unaffordable, but beer and cigarettes never were), she said, "Your dad won't see you anymore. You upset him by singing Cops." Then she laughed joyfully, whether to the actual event or the fact that I wasn't going to see my father anymore, I didn't know.

Before my dad got out of jail, my grandparents convinced Mom to move to Auburn to be closer to her older sister and their family, since Mom couldn't work by then due to her worsening multiple sclerosis, which in turn worsened her drinking and abuse. Also, she'd just given birth to twins—Ava and Elijah—whose parentage my dad outright denied, saying they belonged to one of the many men mom drunkenly had sex with. He could have been right. Who knew?

My grandparents were lovely, elegant people, always quick to smile at us kids. Especially the baby twins, who were strange and beautiful creatures in my eyes. Sometimes I resented them because I was competing with them for mom's already scant attention. But I grew to love them quickly, becoming a mother figure early on during mom's binges and long absences. I'd feed them, bathe them, change their diapers. I was barely six years old.

There was a strange relief to mothering. If I could not be on the receiving end of maternal love, I could at least give it. It was by imitating the acts of motherly love that I began to understand how a mother must feel. I wondered where within my own mom that feeling was hidden. It's difficult to tell if she was lacking of that instinct all her life, or if she just successfully suspended it long enough through a series of getting high that it eventually just dissipated.

My grandparents, so thrilled to rescue their daughter from the evil clutches of the bastard Bob, bought Mom a house to live in with her kids, free of charge. Their only prerequisite? They wanted to spend time with their grandchildren and get to know them, since my dad had never allowed them to while he was on the outside. The miraculous door of familial love had creaked open, a shadowed land completely foreign to me.

In this new scene I found myself in, I was happy for the first time I could remember. We lived in a house that, while small and quaint, was a real *house*, bought and paid for. The thing of dreams. Gone were the days of eviction notices being posted on the door, or landlords angrily swooping in to pack trash bags full of our things and set them outside while Mom was passed out on the couch half naked with a needle in her arm. Now we had a room of our own to fill. Now my half-baked youth could finally rest in joyousness, free-range and complete.

This was going to be good for us, I kept telling myself. I was too young and naïve to realize the depth of depravity I'd already witnessed, but I knew there were some things that made me happy while others did not. Riding my bicycle along the country roads made me happy. The fragrant, cerebral rush of wildflowers melting into one quick vision at the sides of my eyes. Playing games with the baby twins and watching them smile and giggle through their gums, dimples pressed into their porcelain-smooth cheeks. Watching TV with Mom made me happy. Even if she was drinking beer after beer or drugged out of her mind, or both… when no man was present to affect her behavior toward us kids, she was my mom. Mostly. Maybe not my protector or even the most loving person, but she was *mine*. And I loved her for the sole reason that she was the only person I'd ever had in my life until that point. The expansions and contractions of my reality depended upon her completely. She was my north star, even when her eyes were junked up and whited-out to the back of her skull.

These were the things that made me happy, all of which I enjoyed immensely during those first several months living in the new house in Auburn. In addition, people were coming into the house that were not men. Not abusive and mean, or drunk or high or scary. My own family came in to check on us; to play with us. Always quick to smile at my silly questions and the twins' cuteness. For once my child-world was entertained, indulged. The adult world crossed the threshold into mine, instead of the familiar strandedness I felt out in my mother's universe, tugging on a limp arm or matching stares with a strange man.

But Mom's anger and abuse didn't stop. They were merely targeted toward others now, namely my new family, and especially my patient and loving grandparents. I learned a lot about my mother during this time. In disagreements that would arise between her and my grandparents I heard stories of her 'wild youth,' which is what she called it, but according to her parents was far more serious and had never actually ended. It was turmoil and havoc without a graduation date. The grand hour of peaceful integration into responsible adulthood delayed itself year by year, high by high.

Apparently, she had always been an antisocial person, likely having suffered from an undiagnosed mental illness from a very young age. As a child, when they had to go into public she would suffer severe meltdowns, utterly refusing to see anyone. This lasted into her teen years, when she internalized this illness and self-medicated with drugs and alcohol. Although she lacked emotional connections with people—even with her own parents, who hardly knew her—she knew that she was very pretty, and so she used this physical strength as a method to control the boys and men in her life to give her what she wanted. She was determined to leverage any source of power available to her. So many paths to power in my family: gullibility or apoplexy or beauty. So many means to the same self-annihilating end.

Eventually, she started hanging around what my grandparents called 'the bad crowd,' mostly men who drank and did drugs rather than go to school, many of them much older than Mom. While still in high school in the '70s, she and my aunt developed Hepatitis C from sharing dirty heroin needles. There never seemed to be a downturn in her freneticism, only the continuously mounting desire to be filled.

Mom was always looking for the next big high, whether it was from men or drugs. By the time she met my father and had Matthew, she was a full-blown alcoholic with dependency issues—always needing a man around to provide a steady supply of sex, alcohol, and narcotics. Something to soften the world's jagged edges, to dilute the watercolor world. My dad wasn't into drugs, but his alcoholism perfectly complemented her own. They were a match made in heaven. Two slow-rolling heads on the heavenly couch, neglecting the dying flesh of reality. Always a child to attend to, or a festering sore. Always an appetite and the infinite pit of hunger below it.

I rushed through my homework, barely even reading the questions as I filled in the bubbles with my dull pencil—A, then C, then B, then back around again.

"Hurry up," I urged Matthew, who sat across from me with books and papers of his own. "She'll be here soon."

He rolled his eyes and returned to his doodles. "You're so annoying," he muttered.

But I didn't care. It was Wednesday. Wednesdays meant Grandma was coming. After her 12-hour shift at the hospital, she'd drive nearly an hour to our house every week. Her reservoir of time seemed endless, revolving constantly around the care of others.

"GRAMMA!" Ava squealed, having spotted her through the window. I sprang up to meet her at the door, my stomach fluttering as she walked toward me.

"Happy Wednesday!" I cried as she opened the door, wrapping my arms around her cushy middle. I loved the age of her warmth, the staidness of her softness. I loved that there was a steady, dependable sun beyond the contrast of my mother's moods.

She laughed, patting my shoulder. "Happy Wednesday indeed. Gather up the crew, then."

"I want a milkshake this time," Matthew declared as I corralled the twins into their tiny shoes. He was getting to the self-conscious age where even the method by which he consumed ice cream was assailant to his self-image. Thus the kiddie carefree action of licking an ice cream cone was solved by the careful sophistication of a straw. The humiliation of sucking your own fingers clean was an expired concept.

"Milkshake it is," Grandma nodded, rubbing the back of her neck. The gentility of her eyes was qualified by the gravity of weariness, decades of twelve-hour shifts etched onto her expression. I knew she was pretty tired, but that didn't slow me down. Wednesdays were all I had.

"Dairy Queen!" Elijah hollered. I'm not sure he knew what Dairy Queen was—but he knew that when he saw Grandma, he got ice cream.

"Are we gonna watch 7th Heaven after?" I asked. I knew we

were—I just liked to hear her say it. It was my one claim to sureness, my one comfy stake of future.

"Well, don't we always?"

I buckled into the backseat of Gramma's station wagon, closing my eyes. A wave of relief tided my body as the subtle hum of the car released us onto the road, away from the violent unknowing of home life, away from the treacherous coastline that tossed me between land and sea. I sighed, feeling peace for the first time all week. Feeling the precarious truth of that promise stirring sweetly within me: always.

Shortly after the move to Auburn, I was enrolled in Girl Scouts, which, for a reason still unknown to me, was the only extracurricular activity Mom let me take part in. Unfortunately, I hated it almost immediately.

We all had to wear stiff brown dresses, and I hated dresses. At that age I was a tomboy, preferring to hang out with boys and ride my bike, climb trees and go adventuring. Braiding my hair and going door-to-door selling cookies was certainly not my idea of a good time. In retrospect, maybe that's why Mom made me do it—she had always derived a great deal of pleasure from watching people in uncomfortable situations, regardless of whether they were her own kids.

But if I'm being honest, the main reason I hated Girl Scouts was because all the other girls made fun of me relentlessly. Each meet-up, a certain girl would be tasked with bringing the requisite snack. Much to my embarrassment, when it came my turn, my grandmother prepared what she called 'puppy chow,' which I thought was an absolute genius move and all the girls would love me for it—after all, it was Chex Mix soaked in chocolate and peanut butter. What's not to like?

The moment the girls heard the name of my snack, they scrunched their faces up.

"Ew!" Sara cried. "That's disgusting!"

"Dog food!" Jenna shouted, holding her nose.

It felt like something punctured my heart, like a pin in a balloon. The air went out of me and my face went red—I'd never fit in. If the foolproof mélange of chocolate and puppies couldn't win the favors of my feminine peers, nothing could.

"Now, girls," our team leader said, "it's not actual puppy chow. It's really quite delicious." She held a small paper plate, spooning lumps of the brown-black pile into her mouth for effect. "Yummy!"

But no amount of coaxing would convince them to try it. It was a mob mentality: at first only three girls took to making fun of the snack. Then, by default, the rest of the girls wanted nothing to do with it. The hierarchy had already spread itself like a contagion, each girl pulling for higher rank via dramatic disapproval of other people's snacks.

The meeting's activities progressed, the puppy chow sitting untouched in its Tupperware. Although I loved the snack, I didn't take a single bite. It seemed now to be a sure symbol of my otherness, this chunky cube of stew. A combination of all the wrong things, or perhaps all the right things but in the wrong order. Fighting back tears, I pretended to listen to our instructor giving an outdoor skills presentation, but really I was counting down the minutes until I could leave. The moment of my humiliation resounded through my body, contorting my chest in terrible contractions. The immediacy of that feeling would not leave me.

When it was finally over, I packed up the puppy chow as quietly and secretly as I could with tunnel-tight Tupperware vision, but one of the girls spotted me. She came up to me and whispered harshly, her breath hot in my ear: "Enjoy your *puppy chow*, you dog!" Then she laughed before joining her friends, leaving me to stew in the arctic aftermath of her cruelty alone. I threw the snack into the trash and ran all the way home.

That was the beginning of the end. From then on, I was the laughingstock, and I knew there was no coming back. Once, at a park where we were gathered to sell cookies, I was sitting on a bench and we had to put bandanas on. I kept trying but had never done it before, so all the girls made fun of me for being stupid and uncivilized. Another time was at a sleepover at a girl's house, which I had begged Mom to allow me to attend but sorely wished I hadn't, because the whole time I was there the other girls pretended I wasn't there. The few times they spoke to me was to make fun of me. "What does the DOG think about so-and-so?" Or, "Wait, you don't want to upset the dog, do you? Ruff-ruff!"

In no time at all I found myself following in my mother's footsteps: avoiding people, becoming painfully shy and distrustful of others, and seeking ways to manipulate people and situations to get what I wanted. It wasn't so much of a conscious decision to act this way, rather a desperate default in order to survive in the least amount of pain. Soon the same legacy that possessed my mother possessed me too. The feckless abandonment toward discomfort, the uninhibited submergence into landscapes unfamiliar—all for some semblance of joy, or at least numbness.

There were exceptions, of course.

Within the first year of moving to our new house in Auburn, I became friends with a boy named Luke who lived three houses down from us. I was two months older than he was.

That was a disparity worthy of full bragging rights. I was the weathered wise one of the duo, and he my naive companion. His mom, Charlotte, had remarried a man named Peter. I envied what they had—their family reminded me of 7th Heaven. Luke and his siblings were homeschooled, but I would go to his house every chance I got.

Being the new center of my attention, Mom grew increasingly jealous, and in her drunken binges she would rage at Luke. "What are you doing with my daughter? Yes, I'm talking to you, Luke, you dumbass. If you ever get your goddamn prick anywhere near my little girl, I swear to Christ I will fucking hunt you down! You hear me?! Just go the fuck home!"

Understandably, Luke would be brought to tears. We avoided my house as much as we could. I was used to being cursed at and beaten, but this was brand new to him. My mom terrified him.

What drew me to Luke was that he was strange. Like me, he stood out. He was different and didn't have many friends. He would run barefoot along the gravel roads without a care in the world, perfectly content in his loneliness. I admired him for it. It seemed he was keen to some plain-sight secret I couldn't see. This curiosity was the beginning of our closeness.

Admittedly, he had been a good kid before I came along. After having seen so much abuse already and internalized it, I began lashing out at the world. It started with me convincing Luke that it was perfectly acceptable to hide in the bushes and throw rocks at moving vehicles. This, looking back, was probably some poorly-sublimated re-appropriation of power—smashing the property of strangers. For all I knew, their lives were easier, loftier than my own. They drove big cozy cars to beautiful anonymous places with smiling anonymous families. How much harm could be caused by a sonic smash to the windshield? It's not like getting smacked in the face in real-time, or burned to hot flesh by the cigarette of a psychopath bedding your mother.

The first time we did it, the car stopped. Luke froze, and I left him—ran off like my life depended on it. I'd seen enough violence to know about its aftermath, and it usually centered around raging red-faced adults moving quickly my way. The only reaction available to me was to frantically flee in the opposite direction. I thought he'd follow, but he didn't—I left poor Luke there in the dust.

He never told a soul I was involved. It was then I knew I could trust him.

The first time we kissed was in my backyard. I was in midsentence, rambling on about how to properly light firecrackers, when Luke quickly leaned in and pecked me on the lips. I jumped back, shocked by the foreign feeling of his lips, dry and salty, on my own. We both giggled nervously, saying nothing. Then he ran home abruptly, his little bare feet slapping the Texan dirt.

"Wait, where are you going?"

But he didn't answer, didn't even look back. He kicked up small aerials of dust like a Roadrunner mid-mission. Soon he disappeared from my view completely, and the wind had wiped his footsteps clean.

Later, I'd learn he ran home to tell his mom he was going to marry me. We were seven years old.

My dad was out of jail for several months before he requested a visit from us. When Mom told us, Matthew looked away from the television, his eyes alight.

"Really?"

"Really," Mom spat. Her eyes were obsidian, full of electricity. It was hard to get a grasp on how she felt about anything. Despite her intermittent histrionic outbursts, there remained steeled inside her some nebulous secret. Something I could never get to. Something deeply forbidden.

When it came to a subject as ripe as my father, all extremes of demeanor were possible. Matthew's earnest hopefulness landed flat and two-dimensional beside my wariness. I was skeptical of this man, whose absence allotted free reign for strange, shadowy men to stumble stoned around the house, lost souls looking for a toilet to piss on. But if Mom was willing to see him, then I was going with her. Some blind sense of loyalty deployed me to her side continually. This was but another reckless endeavor that had come to make up my childhood track record. Another whim to endure by proxy of Mom's manic mind.

She drove us past the outskirts of our old town to his RV on a muggy summer night, the rushing air matted with mosquitos and cigarette smoke from the perpetual pull of Mom's bad habit. I let my hands dangle outside the window and looked up toward the dusk. The meltdown of the sun pitched up the crooked tent of night, stucco stars in suspension. It was as if they, too, were anxiously awaiting the reunion of those two grisly forces. Only they seemed better equipped to witness it. I was without their safety-net of lightyear distances, without their calm aloofness.

Mom threw her cigarette stub out onto the dirt and stepped out of the car. The tawny light coming from the trailer made her seem like a daguerreotype, garish and unreal. She sighed, knowing exactly what she was about to get into.

"Well," she said, "Should we see how the bastard's doing?"

We climbed up the rusted metal steps into the living room, an aluminum oven of dank air and hot furniture that stuck to the bottom of my thighs made a sucking sound every time I shifted my bodyweight. The place was littered with loose tobacco and empty beer cans and harbored a sour smell of bodies in senescence. It was a familiar sight to me—scenes of squalor and electric air, frenetic still with the remnants of some recent drunken rage.

Mom looked around the place with haughty gingerness, "Doing well for yourself, I see."

"Sure am," Dad said, sipping a beer, perched at the tenuous matrix of calmness that replaced the rage of sobriety but preceded the rage of dissolution. They made some other codified aggressions toward each other before shooing us out.

I sat on the foldout table outside of the trailer, sweat dewing on my forehead, while Mom and Dad had sex behind the thin plywood door of the bedroom. By this time, I was used to such things. It didn't seem any better or any worse that it was my own father contributing to such a chorus. He was just another man—faceless and brutal, and treated my mother just the same as any other stranger.

I passed the time by playing with the twins, who laughed and cooed with their plastic toys, ignorant of the meaning of the grunts and hollers resounding from within. They were giggly, reveling in their innocence that had already abandoned me. I felt the gravity of knowledge pressing down upon me, the slow weight of realization. I looked at the twins and felt sorrowful for them. Their easy brightness was always overshadowed by the disconsolation of our mother. Above the glittering veneer of their vision rung the terrible sounds of a miserable woman. I sang them silly songs to compete with the noise, lullabies I had heard and half-remembered, and worked their names into it for my own amusement.

"Ava-Ava bo-Bava fee-fi fo-Fava! Ava! A-a-Ava!"

Beside me, Matthew whittled a stick into a fine point. "Dad's the best," he said earnestly, mostly to himself, soaked in the glory of his homemade reality. I didn't bother to correct him, since the alternative wasn't true either. Side by side we stewed inside two polar atmospheres, glued together by the cheap shell of the family unit.

After an unending stretch of time, their two silhouettes stumbled out of the trailer, finishing the incoherent tail-end of a hostile conversation.

"You chicken shit! You think you can talk to me like that? Makes you feel like a big man, huh?"

"I can talk to you however I damn please, ya dumb bitch."

"Just get in the car. Kids, you too."

We piled into the van, a debauched Noah's ark raging into the Texan night. The twins cried as Mom swerved all over the road, steaming with fury and five hours of liquor. I tried to calm them, but it was a task that could not be completed. Their faces only reddened in sync with Mom and Dad's.

"Christ! You're gonna get us arrested, woman!" Dad hollered.

"Then you fucking drive!" The orange suns of their cigarettes swung with force as they screamed at each other, little wisps of ashes seizing into the back of the car and dusting up my eyes. Matthew just sat silently looking out the window, a stone statue waiting for the blizzard to pass.

"I don't wanna," Dad said in his low-croak fashion, taking another swig of beer as if to distinguish the end of this declaration.

"Then play with your kids and shut the fuck up!" Mom kept taking dire drags of her cigarette as if her life depended on it, the way she always did when she was raging. I watched as the thick finger of orange ember crawled closer to her lips. Her face looked unnaturally pale against its faint glow, a wax candle slowly melting to nothingness.

"Half of 'em aren't even mine!" Dad said.

I remember thinking that was strange for him to say, as I didn't think it mattered much. Any pride he might have harbored over his blood children manifested in either complete neglect or drunken spectacles of assault. He chugged the rest of the bottle and threw it out of the window. I heard the glass splatter into a thousand mirrors, reflecting a choir of filthy faces.

It was official: Dad had re-entered our lives.

CHAPTER 3

That September, right after the school year started, Matthew and I were throwing bang snaps against the driveway after dinner. The little *crack* never failed to please me—it was like glass popping, or a bone breaking. There was great satisfaction in the booming accomplishment of such scarce effort. The effect was direct and immediate, a subconscious way to measure the efficacy of my impact on the surrounding world. So far I had yet to influence anything that cost more than 99 cents at the convenience store.

"Matthew!" Mom screamed from inside. He ran in immediately—we both knew not to keep Mom waiting. Eager to see him get in trouble, I followed. I thought maybe she'd cuss him out for leaving piss on the toilet seat or forgetting to put the milk back into the fridge. Or perhaps something more inventive this time, since she was always contriving new angles to get upset with him.

"Tomorrow after school," she said as soon as we entered, "We're going uptown. You're gonna be famous." She held up a floppy white piece of paper, waving it through the air. Her face was twisted up into some slightly concerning strain of ecstasy, as if any slight perturbance would spiral her into either abject dejection or abject neuroses. That was the horror of Mom's happiness—the source of it was always obscene, which made her personality so precarious. Every tiny revelation had the capacity to be either the apocalypse or the rapture.

“Sweet,” Matthew said.

“Why would Matthew be famous?” I asked, suspicious.

“The local station wants him to audition for some TV commercial. Eight-to-twelve-year-old boys from town.” She put the letter on the counter and continued to scan it as she lit a cigarette. Something of herself must have emerged from that paper. Some glimpse at what could have been, some wholesome image of herself that never came to fruition.

But to me, the idea of Matthew on television was preposterous, unfathomable. That a camera would deign to indulge the dumb oval of his indifferent face angered me. What special quality did he obtain that was not already plentiful within me? I swallowed my jealousy, watching him run back out the door, screen banging closed behind him. Apparently the notion of stardom was unmoving to him. I heard the unmistakable popping of bang snaps continuing to strike the asphalt, the tired ritual of a boy contented to his tiny powers.

I sat in a cushioned waiting room chair with Mom on one side of me and Matthew on the other. The room was crawling with prepubescent boys and hawking mothers leering sideways at their competition. Some looked nervous, but most looked like Matthew—playing Gameboys and looking at magazines. I watched them indignantly—these drooling dummies completely impervious to the gravity of this situation, selected for the coincidental miracle of being eight-to-twelve. I crossed my arms and scowled at them.

A woman popped her head into the room. “Nicholas?”

A blonde little boy and his mother stood up and followed the woman into the adjoining room. The mother made a clanking sound as she heeled out into the hallway in stilettos. I looked to my Mom's feet, her improvised black flats all peeled off at the heels. Her resident aura of Marlboros; the harsh breath.

Less than five minutes passed before she appeared again, dispensing Nicholas and his mother back into the waiting room. "Matthew?" She might as well have called my own name. It was the only time where being within the vicinity of my brother was close to a life of glamour.

I excitedly followed Mom and Matthew through the door and sat in a less comfortable folding chair against the wall. The place where it all began. I squirmed on the sideline while Matthew stood in the middle of the room, a camcorder pointing right at his face. At the opposite end of the room sat a man and woman behind a desk, the qualification system for nubile talent. The woman was unlike my mother, like all of the other women here—seamless and hopeful, and when they spoke it was with a cool assurance. The man beside her shuffled papers, hair molting into an amicable baldness. Authority gleamed upon his eyeglasses as he looked up. "Okay, Matthew. Can you say, *Mom, what's for dinner?*"

"Mom, what's for dinner."

He squinted, wrote something down. "One more time?"

"Mom. What's for dinner?"

"Thanks, Matthew." The man nodded then glanced up at

me, paused as if to absorb my potentialities. “Is this your sister?”

“Yes,” Mom said quickly, squeezing her hands on my shoulders. “This is little Emma.”

There was a pause as the man and woman looked at each other, exchanging what I assumed to be prophetic expressions of my future. “Emma, would you like to try it?”

I smiled and stood up. “Mom, what’s for dinner?”

“Would you come stand over here?”

I moved to where Matthew was, forcing him out of the way so the camera was on me alone. Finally, I could offer redemption to the uninspired effort of my brother. “Mom, what’s for dinner?” I flashed the camera my best smile. They smiled back.

“Emma, would you like to be on television?”

On the drive home, Mom shook her head in amazement, giggling at the steering wheel. She kept flicking her head back to me as if to confirm my newfound utility. “Out of all those kids, Emma, you got it! You beat ‘em!”

Matthew, sitting in the seat in front of me, was silent. In the rearview mirror, I could see him, arms crossed, eyes narrowed.

“Aw, what is it, Mattie? Upset that your sister’s a better actor than you? Well, get over it! You’re acting like a pussy.”

I could tell this stung him. He gazed out the window, and in the mirror I saw a tear rolling down his cheek. He quickly brushed it away. He held his emotions within the tremulous line of his lip, liable to quake under pressure.

Mom hated him. Well, he hated her back. Too bad for him, he could have found redemption in annexing a purpose Mom found valuable. Like funneling money and garnering social respect. He narrowly missed his window, slumped deeper into his seat until the seatbelt reached his nose.

Of course, I wasn't able to do the commercial anyway. It was one of those auditions in which you had to pay a company to represent you in order to take part, and we didn't have the money. Mom didn't tell me right away; not out of sympathy, but because she was in a drunken haze for three straight days and didn't check the mail during those episodes. So, naturally, I found Luke as soon as I could and declared that I was going to be famous.

He frowned at me, picking a little scab on his arm he'd earned while climbing trees. "What in God's name are you talking about?" he asked, spitting onto the dirt for emphasis.

I grabbed him by the shoulders dramatically and shook him. "Are you even listening to me? I'm going to be famous, Luke! I'm gonna star in a commercial that's going to be seen by *millions*!" I stared off into the distance, my eyes glazed over in wonderment. "I'm gonna leave this ole town behind and say goodbye to everything I've ever known. I'm gonna be a star, in TV commercials, then in the shows and the movies! I'll live in Hollywood and be chauffeured in a cherry red Corvette convertible."

Luke looked frightened. "You're leaving?"

"Of course I am!" A mirage of futures welled up within me, each riper than the next.

He said nothing for a few moments. Then, innocently and without meeting my gaze, he asked, "Can I come with you?" He had dirty, squinty eyes, always watching for something significant. Something about his scrub-hard attitude made him unique; his wildness.

I grasped his collar and gave him a big smooch on the mouth, just like I'd seen in the movies. "Yes, you idiot! Why do you think I'm telling you all this?" There we were, the connection of all our dreaming. Here was the beginning, here our baseless threshold to betterness.

Then we strolled down the street, arm in arm, waving goodbye to everything we'd ever known, because we were going to blow out of town. I was going to be a somebody. A lady in lipstick and high heels, breezing off to important places. There was going to be life as I had never fathomed before, where the dust was dethroned by diamonds.

I was going to be a star.

Matthew shoved the phone toward our cousin William, mischief sparkling in his eyes.

"Go ahead, Willie boy," he said.

William took the phone, looking hesitant, looking toward the door to scout for any impending adult footsteps.

"911," Matthew commanded.

Slowly, William pressed 9.

"Hurry up!" I urged, hungry for some excitement. The three of us were holed up in Grandma and Grandpa's bedroom, hiding from the grownups. The air was stifled, displaced by our soda breaths as we squirmed around the sweaters and magazines. William pressed himself into a corner for better coverage.

He finished dialing and held the phone to his ear. I heard a muffled, "911, what is your emergency?"

He immediately slammed the phone back onto the receiver, his eyes wild with terror. "They answered," he said weakly, face flushing like a fold.

"Duh!" Matthew laughed.

The next moment, the phone started to ring. In the hall, I heard Aunt Renee, William's mom, pick up. Matthew and I returned to our work of thinking up some trouble to start or a rule to break while William brooded silently with his legs crossed. He looked like a sinner fresh out of morning mass.

Aunt Renee raised her kids by the book, especially William, who was a month younger than me. He had to be more careful than Matthew and I did. Whatever sort of propriety he was enlisted to was beyond our roguish awareness.

Suddenly the door burst open and Aunt Renee grabbed William by the ear, dragging him into the next unoccupied room. He didn't struggle, resigned to a fate he signed on for by fact of being our cousin. He was a prime target for the sublimations of our childish filtration systems. The badness of home always found a way to convolute everything outside of it.

Matthew and I pressed our ears to the wall and listened while she beat him relentlessly. He wailed and screamed for what felt like an eternity. I cringed, feeling for his familiar pain but relishing the anomaly of being on the other side of a beating. Matthew remained at the wall, but I moved away after a few minutes and pretended to be busy with something in the closet. It was never possible to get used to a noise like that, despite its regularity. Easier to pretend until something changed, or stopped.

That's not to say Aunt Renee was a bad parent; she wasn't. She was just a strict disciplinarian. Believe me, I'd gotten far more and much worse beatings of my own. I envied William's upbringing. He had nice clothes and a pool in his backyard. He had birthdays attended by other kids, and plenty of presents. His mother adored him. Unlike the pathological oddity of my mother, whatever discipline he endured was not only given by love, but sourced from it.

William was strictly forbidden from watching PG-13 material; even the Simpsons were off-limits. Meanwhile I was being force-fed the scariest horror movies that would give me nightmares for years to come: films like The Exorcist, Hellraiser, Scream. Mom had a perverse obsession with horror and the macabre, and she did not want to experience them alone, so she always made me sit down and watch them with her, sometimes even prying my hands off my eyes when a particularly disturbing scene would occur: "No! You have to watch!" she'd say.

While watching Hellraiser for the first time, I ran to her

during a particularly gruesome scene. She laughed with great pleasure, pushing me away. Of course, my feelings were hurt—all I wanted was to be comforted, but such a thing was rare with my mother. There was a perpetual film of detachment around her, keeping her from me. And when those same horror movies started appearing in my dreams and I'd wake up crying, Mom always hollered the same two words through the wall: *"Shut up!"*

There was an element of sadism at play here. Not only was she in love with horror as a personal taste, but she also garnered satisfaction by inflicting terror on others. This manifested itself in a list of perverse jokes played at my expense.

"Emma, come here," she said one night after I'd brushed my teeth for bed. I followed her to my bedroom doorway. "What is that?" she asked, pointing into the room.

I squinted into the darkness. "I don't see anything."

"There, under the bed!" She shoved me inside and slammed the door. Matthew promptly emerged from under my bed in a Freddy Kreuger mask, hands contorting into the air as if to slash all the invisible throats, leading up to my own. I screamed, struggling with the doorknob—but Mom held the door closed with her body weight so I couldn't escape. The terror of betrayal seized me in the small darkness. Matthew growled, reaching out for me, and I shrieked 'til my throat burned. The louder I cried, the harder Mom laughed.

After a couple of minutes, the novelty wore off, and Mom moved away from the door. She leaned against the hallway in post-ecstasy. "Why do you do this to me?" I demanded at last, squaring off against her in the hallway, my face hot with tears. I thought the grim confrontation of my misery might offset her, might stir up some dormant speck of sympathy. That surely there must be a saturation point to my suffering and its petty amusements.

She only sighed toward me with a frivolous boredom and said, "Because it's fun." There was a strange look to her eyes, like a rabid creature in slow wake.

This same behavior played out in other ways as well. Sometimes she just liked to target me for embarrassment, such as the time when all the neighborhood kids were playing in my front yard and she stumbled outside in her stained bathrobe. I knew at first glance that she was raging drunk. "Get your ass in the fucking house!" she screamed. "And the rest of you, LEAVE!"

I watched as my friends' eyes widened, shooting glances toward each other. They quickly turned and slinked off, probably to play in a normal kid's yard. I was humiliated that yet another normalcy evaded me by means of my mother. Just an hour before Mom had told me it was fine to have them over.

Inside, I didn't bother to question her reasoning—I knew there was none. Her logic was strange and unassailable. To live under its dominant rule was to perform a perpetual series of contortions. There was always the anxiety of waiting for when the hammer would strike down on the hot iron of my happiness.

The next big embarrassment came a couple of weeks later when Erma Nash Intermediate School hosted a Luau dance for the kids. I was nervous about the prospect of dressing up and dancing with everyone, but I was excited too. It was another chance at being part of the collective, of elusive acceptance. Of course, it was Hawaiian-themed, so I found a lei in the Halloween costume box. I was going to wear my bright pink top with flip-flops to show off my stylistic savviness. Perhaps if puppy chow couldn't win them over then my fashionable sensibilities could.

"What the fuck is that?" Mom snapped when I came out of my room in my outfit, deflating my aura like a rigged kite in a glass fight.

"My Hawaiian costume," I said simply.

"It's a *dance,* Emma. Go put on your white dress," she mumbled through a lit cigarette, snapping toward my room.

"But it's Hawaiian-themed—"

"Emma, go!"

My chest burned with that familiar blend of anger and sadness. It was so frustrating to never understand what was going on. To be made to do things with no explanation. To endlessly teeter beneath her cold thumb like a TV channel switched on and off.

I changed into my frilly white church dress for fear of being beaten otherwise. I stuffed the lei into the waistband of my underwear, planning to slip it on at the dance. There was always a way to worm around the fear. Living with it constantly creates industrious children, but usually at the expense of a black eye or bruised shins. I tried not to itch my waist as the plastic flowers scratched against me, a reminder of my awfulness.

Thirty minutes later, Mom dropped me off at the school. I entered the gymnasium with my head down, but it was already happening—the laughing. I prayed there was some horribly-dressed dweeb close within my proximity, but it looked like I was the only one.

"Didn't you hear it's Hawaiian-themed, Emma?" cackled a girl in a grass skirt and yellow tank top.

"Are you a flower girl?" laughed another. They turned toward each other, squaring me off like a foreign flank. I felt my otherness stretch like a clouded landscape, raw and immediate from every coordinate. Heat rushed up my face and I scuttled away to a less populated corner of the gym.

I sat on the bleachers and tried to be invisible, watching as the flocks of girls unfolded the hackneyed ceremony of popularity. It seemed so natural to them, this unspoken ordinance of knowing what to say and when, who to disdain and why, how to act and react. Every move I made was preordained to be the wrong one. I dropped my lei and rubbed it in the ground with my shoe-sole, watching it collect dirt. I would never, ever be allowed to feel happy.

On the first day of fifth grade, each student was accompanied by a parent to their seats. I sat with my hands nervously folded on my lap and watched how the rest of the world operated its regular adults. They introduced themselves to the teacher as part of a rite of investment in the future of their child's education. My mother stood beside me like a foolish idol, bored and out of place. She didn't even *try* to learn from these normal parents. She was always so brazen in her divergence from everyone else, in a way that I sometimes secretly admired but mostly despised. It seemed she attracted every opportunity to showcase this disparity.

I pointed out to her the bizarre inscriptions on the white board, narrowing my gaze in a vain attempt to decode the strangeness. "What is that?" I asked, looking up to her.

"You don't know what cursive is?" she asked in disgust. "My god, you're so stupid."

The kids around me ducked their heads, pretending not to have heard. Once again I was flagged for my otherness: being stupid or tasteless or the offspring of an unhinged woman. The sea of desks retreated in my mind until I was at the apex, bobbed and stunned. I looked up at the teacher, tears in my eyes, hoping for her to say, *Don't worry, Emma—we're going to learn it this year.*

Instead, she shuffled some papers on her desk. I guess I really was stupid.

My dad eventually rented a trailer in our old town, and Matthew and I would visit every so often. But for the first couple of years, he refused to let the twins join us.

Mom's boyfriend Tim stepped up and treated the twins as his own. He was at every birthday party—it actually looked like he cared about them. Though I didn't love Tim, even as a kid, I could appreciate what he did for the twins. They were just babies, and I knew enough to know that they needed some kind of love. I also was dimly aware that somehow my love was not enough, that it needed to be sourced in a provenance older and wiser than me. Even when I loved the twins tenderly, I knew it was somehow different than the cold crumbs of affection given to them by Mom. There was something I could not give them, something that resided solely within her. I hoped Tim could accomplish it.

One day when I was in Dad's trailer watching television with Matthew, he came through the door with a woman I had never seen before. She was pretty, with long blonde hair and blue eyes—but she looked filthy. I'd always had a hard time reconciling beauty with squalor. But pretty women all over the world were poor, and talked and smoked like men. They were a fascinating species to me. Every female face I met bore some similarities of Mom in one way or another. Dirt on the feet and panic in the eyes. Clothing frayed at the edges and knuckles cracked from dust and dryness.

"These are the kids," Dad mumbled as he disappeared down the hallway. I heard the mouth of the fridge suction open then shut, the clink of beers inside their bottles before some wind of anger burst them to pieces.

The lady bent down and smiled at me. She smelled like smoke, and her makeup was smudged all black and blue around her eyes. "Hey honey, how many siblings do you have?" Her teeth were yellowed and sticky, kept pinching onto the corners of her lips at the end of every word. I wanted to offer her something to eat but felt afraid to ask. I got to learn after a while that there was a threshold of language that belonged exclusively to the adults, such as cursing or making offerings of hospitality or making crude remarks publicly.

"Four," I told her. I glanced at Matthew—he never looked away from the screen, his face lit up blue by some commercial like a doltish moon in waning.

Dad emerged from the hall with eyes like daggers. "What did you just say?"

"I said there's four of us, Daddy. Me, Matthew, and the twins." I looked up toward him as he loomed toward me, a bumbling liquid phantom.

He lunged for me, slapping me in the face and then the head once I'd covered my face with my hands. "You're lying! Why are you lying?"

It seemed as though Matthew didn't notice. The woman had moved into the kitchen—so as not to interfere, I guess. This was not an earth-shattering revelation to her—that a man could refuse the kids he created while abusing the others he could claim.

"Why are you hitting me?" I sobbed. "Please stop it!"

I had no idea that he didn't want anyone to know about the twins. How could I? I was just a kid. Their existence was just as intertwined with my father's as mine was. The same hatred my mother had for Matthew found itself a home in my father, too. I guess I was the lucky one, standing between two rifts of hatred.

Unfortunately, this carried on throughout the twins' lives. My dad never bought them anything or learned anything about them. To him they were nagging extensions of some other man's fun night out. The twins didn't like him either. They cried a lot when they eventually were made to stay with him, and trying to comfort them was often futile. I didn't blame them—he was scary. He didn't turn on cartoons—we watched the news and black and white John Wayne films. The television at least was a mandated outlet of violence. All the blood and death and sadistic triumph of the pictures curdled in my brain. All of it plastered thickly onto the tenuous youth of the twins, sucking in second-hand smoke from sunrise to sundown.

His house was more of a man cave than a home. It was dark and dreary; all the pictures were of Budweiser and naked women. The counters were stiff with sticky substances and moldered with leftover food. Our beds were disgusting hand-me-downs full of urine stains. We were too grossed out to even use the blankets because they were never washed and would leave residues all over. Everything smelled like pee from his poorly-trained dogs that smothered the place over with an awful smell of oil and body odor. Sometimes I would slip on drying puddles of piss and smack my head against the flat breasts of a pinup girl.

He was a dirty man. Being a mechanic, his hands were always black, his fingernails caked with dirt and grime. I never wanted him to touch me—not that he ever did. But whenever he was close to me I was repelled by the smell of him—stale beer and sweat and grime. Not owning a toothbrush, his yellowed, rotting teeth went unbrushed. There was no soap in the house aside from the dish soap for the sink, but even that was rarely used: "The water will kill the germs," he'd say. Not hot water: *water*.

My dad was small and slim, never fat, and wore loose Wrangler jeans and white tee shirts from Dollar General. He never washed them, let alone our clothing, so eventually his clothes would be so caked with dirt, oil and grime that they would stiffen like cardboard and repel anyone he got near. He was a noxious substance, reeking always of wrath or piss or Budweiser. Even after all these years, I can't recall a single memory of him showering. His trailer reeked of cigarettes; its walls yellowed from nicotine stains just like the gnarled tips of his fingers. It was its own self-containing air of rankness and sadness.

My dad was also a very heavy drinker. He could finish two 24 packs between 5 a.m. and 6 p.m. Then he'd go to sleep, which is why we were never fed. This was the only similarity that loosely bonded him to my mother all those years. Their schedules of absolute intoxication were perfectly aligned. Both feared a world above the scuba-vision of drunkenness; of dry sobriety and its resident responsibilities.

He never liked any of us, except for Matthew, who relished his attention, spending long hours at the shop learning how to work on cars while my dad drank beer and told overexaggerated stories about 'loose women.' Pretty soon Matthew was his little puppy dog, dutifully following him around wherever he went. The image of his future was completely contingent upon Dad; whatever arbitrary shape my father assumed was the shape Matthew wanted to be absorbed by. He was no match against the glorified model of our father.

On vacations that we were unlucky enough to have to spend with my dad, they were inseparable while I alone tended to the twins, bathing them, changing their diapers, and feeding them on the rare occasions I was given access to the fridge, on which my dad had installed a padlock. I'm not sure why, though; aside from milk and some random condiments, the fridge was usually empty. All the good food, like chips and snacks, was stored inside my dad's bedroom bureau, where none of us—not even Matthew—dared to venture.

When I looked in the mirror, I often didn't recognize the tired eyes that stared back at me. They looked like the eyes of a mother who had spent decades ignored and overworked. They looked scrubbed and spectral, like the negative of an abandoned photograph. I bent closer to my double, fogging up her distorted face breath by breath. Better not to confront the stale face of exhaustion. Better not to see how the time had reduced me to this flat duplicate.

I was 12.

CHAPTER 4

"Do you ever wonder what the world would be like without parents?" Luke asked.

It was late afternoon, and huge cotton candy clouds were drifting by as we lazed on the grass below them. A cool breeze passed over us, ruffling our clothes, before retreating to the backyards to dry the laundry flapping on clotheslines.

"All the time," I told him with more honesty than he realized. "Why?"

Luke had a puzzled look on his face, his eyebrows knitted together. He always had this look when he was thinking deeply about something: dodgeball strategies, history class, and girls, to name a few.

"Cause without parents, what would we do? All us kids."

I laughed at the thought. "We'd rule the world, of course."

Luke nodded; his eyebrows still furrowed. I could tell this notion fascinated him. "But then we'd grow up and become parents ourselves. So I guess it's impossible to have a world without parents."

"Nah, not really. We could for a little while. It would just go away."

"Right," he agreed.

Something was bothering him, I could tell. But I didn't know how to ask. Thankfully, I didn't have to.

"You're acting funny," he said at last, and I knew that was it. By now he was attuned to my changes. There was no being subtle around him.

I turned to him. "No, I'm not."

"Uh huh. You're acting different now."

"Since when?" I was defensive, my hackles up.

"Since the other day," he said casually, not meeting my eye. "You seem... sad."

Damn, he was good.

"Why are you sad?" he asked. But I said nothing in response. "Your mom?"

Yes. Exactly. My mom. The one who steadily fed the madness that shucked away at our lives; the one who opened our home to variform abuse, and reopened it. But of course, I couldn't tell him that, because then I would have to tell him what I saw, and she made me promise not to tell *anyone*. To make impervious the perverse Pandora's box, the purgatory of lifelong silence. But that didn't stop him from prying.

"What'd she do *this* time?"

Hot tears formed in my eyes. I brushed them away, my jaw tightening. "It's not what *she* did."

Images seared into my mind: a man coming into the house

and talking with my mom. He was the uncle of a classmate from school who would sometimes come to my house to play with me. He would pick her up and bring her home. But this time was different. This time he dropped by even though his niece was not at my house, and very soon after, my mom started screaming. We watched helplessly as he pulled off her pants while she thrashed and yelled. He shoved her against the back door and raped her there in the living room while my siblings and I watched.

I tried to cover the twins' eyes with my hands but they kept looking to see why their mom was screaming, their little eyes filled with confusion and fear. Mom tried to kick the back door open to escape, but I could see she didn't stand a chance. After a few minutes, Matthew ran into the living room with a baseball bat and chased the man outside, where he hopped a fence and took off.

Mom sank to the floor and wept. I went over to her while she pulled her pants up, but she immediately stood up and went into her bedroom, slamming the door behind her.

The next day at school I marched right up to the girl whose uncle it was and shoved her to the ground.

"Your uncle raped my mom!" I declared, trembling with anger.

"You liar!" she said, scrambling to collect her spilled papers.

Another girl named Destiny helped her up, horrified by my behavior. "You're a terrible friend!" she told me, then whisked her away with me standing there alone. I would never speak to them again. A police report would never be filed, and I would be forbidden from speaking of it altogether. Another trauma to erase, to shove between the perishing branches of family history. It sunk me with a sick gravity to carry this with me, like stomaching a sour fruit.

"Oh, come on," Luke pleaded. "What is it? You can talk to me."

I shook my head and stared at the sky. Put away the memory for another day, some tragic chapter to collect dust. A good daughter absorbs then buries the traumas of her mother. Preserves the complexes of her mother in the breeding ground of hereditary resignation.

"Nothing," I told him, and in my heart I truly believed it. It *was* nothing. Like so many of the things I had already seen, this was yet another unremarkable stain on the pages of my family's story. Like most things, it would be forgotten. The wound would heal and fade, and new wounds would replace it. They, too, would heal and be forgotten. This was the cycle of lost things. Things that not only disappeared but had to be forgotten entirely, lest they come back to haunt us. Because if they weren't forgotten, then how could we ever live with ourselves?

Mom was the greatest testament to that. She was a walking collection of lost things. I didn't know it at the time, but you could see it in her eyes, and in the very depth of her being. That ghastly hunger, that dead electricity. She was the fulcrum for the spinning compass of broken spirits that surrounded her, the freshwater Lethe of oblivion. A place to lose yourself, a blank page for the fugue state. She herself was lost, so all of these experiences, these people—wasn't it all just a natural byproduct that they would be lost and forgotten as well?

Such is what I told myself, and therefore what I did not tell Luke.

He looked at me, confused. “What do you mean, nothing?”

“It’s nothing,” I told him. “Really. Just... nothing.”

CHAPTER 5

I used to love going to Blockbuster—what kid didn't? The colorful shelves lined with every movie imaginable. Every possible story, uplifted through music and dancing and vibrant pixels. We could pick out a family movie and watch it together on Saturday night. Maybe we'd even get popcorn or Twizzlers. And when I fell asleep on the couch, my dad would carry me to my bed.

That's the kind of life I suspected other kids were probably living. But not me.

"Go, go!" Mom hissed, waving me toward the door. I hurried off while Mom pretended to browse foreign films.

Near the entrance, concealed behind the candy shelves, sat a shopping cart full to the very top with movies. Like I'd done dozens of times before, I grabbed on and pushed it out the door.

Under the sunshine, the shiny VHS cases glinted with all the colors of the rainbow. I felt like a champ, an instant-harvester of chattel valued by my mother. It was a swooping accomplishment when executed correctly since it watered the cinematic union between us. I could barely see over the mountain of stolen movies as I strolled through the parking lot. I didn't know where the van was, so I just kept on walking. The dim awareness that there might be some prime emotional disturbance opportunities in these movies for her to inflict upon me only gave me slight pause.

"Emma, get to the goddamn van!"

Obediently, I followed Mom's voice. She snatched the cart from my hands and began to shovel the movies into the backseat. I grabbed as many as I could, dumping armfuls onto the seat. I tried to be helpful. To make her proud of me. Make myself symmetrical to her, even in her badness.

In my pocket, my most recent Dollar General purchase banged against my leg. I smiled. It was a wooden angel, a wire halo perched atop its head. Fun-sized divinity.

Whenever Dad gave me money, I went to Dollar General and bought presents for Mom. I loved bringing gifts home to her. That's how she showed us love, so that's the way I knew how to show love too. The house was littered with cheap, poorly made knick-knacks. Every shelf, every table, every corner. It made me feel like she might actually love me. Her language of affection was condensed into these little idols, an alphabet I closely observed and desperately spelled.

I had browsed the store with my four dollars in hand, the world my oyster. I could buy anything—a wreath of plastic leaves and red foam berries, or a picture frame with gold edges—gold! But lined up on a lower shelf were several wooden figurines—a cat, a bird, a small jewelry box—but for Mom, the angel. It had long hair and hands folded in front. It reminded me of her.

"EMMA! GET IN THE GODDAMN VAN!"

I got in the passenger seat, heart inevitably fluttering. Her anxiety leaked onto mine like sap. She was backing up before I had even closed my door, bumping into the shopping cart we'd left in the parking lot.

"I got something for you," I said, excitement bubbling up in a slow appeal to her affection. I reached into my pocket, imagining the expression of adoration soon to occur.

"You what?" Her eyes were wide as she started the car, knuckles white. She was frazzled. Drunk, probably.

I held the angel toward her in the palm of my hand. It looked as beautiful to me as any fancy sculpture in a museum, a regular Venus de Milo.

"Hey!" A man in a blue vest called, emerging from Blockbuster. He ran toward us, wagging his finger. "Hey, you ladies better stop!"

"Shit!"

The tires screeched as Mom ripped into the road. I scrambled to buckle my seatbelt, the movies sliding across the backseat. I turned around to get a good glimpse of our semi-victory, which just looked like a tired forty-year-old-man huffing over his knees. I knew being caught just meant we'd go to a different Blockbuster next time. It didn't bother Mom. So it didn't bother me either.

The angel had fallen from my hand and now rested at my feet, her halo snapped off and nowhere to be seen. Suddenly it was just a... person. De-winged and molted, stupid. Some holy little lie rolling around in the dirt. Looking at it welled the salt of sorrow into my stomach. I slouched against the window and watched the dull film roll.

"Where are we going?" I asked as we passed by our road.

"Mechanic."

While the van was being worked on, I scoured the floor for the wire halo. When I found it, I held it to her head. Maybe I could glue it. Did we have any glue? Maybe I could squeeze it onto her head, but then she just looked like some defeated thespian with a flashy headband.

"Get in the back," Mom snapped. "Don is coming home with us."

The mechanic sat silently in the front seat. He was filthy, smelling the car up with oil and gas. It seemed to me that every man shared the same base mephitic odor, varying only slightly in undertones. Alcohol and crud in exponential embodiments. Beer or whiskey, oil or soot—all absorbed by the hard, angry body of men in emotional crises. Father or stranger. My mother was their humidifier. Exactly like them—but a *woman*. A promise.

At home, Mom took Don in and pointed toward the yard. "You stay out here," she told me. Then she pushed Matthew out too. "Both of you stay out here."

Slam.

This wasn't the first time something like this had happened. I understood Mom by then—if I asked her a question, she would answer in great detail. Matthew and I knew not to go in. It was likely we'd be out here for hours. We drank from the hose if we got thirsty.

I looked at the windows from the yard, entertaining the

tired series of possibilities. She was likely sleeping with Don to pay for the oil change. Or maybe he was giving her ecstasy or heroin.

It was a nice spring day, so Matthew and I were content enough to sit on the steps and draw in the dirt. But some days, in the summer, it was too hot, or we were hungry, and we pounded on the door, begging her to let us in. Sometimes she was passed out drunk—other times she just ignored us.

"I'm bored," I said finally, trying not to think about the angel and its fall from grace. "Wanna go to Barbara's?"

Matthew shrugged and stood up, which I took to mean that he was bored too, and probably hungry. We walked across the street to Barbara's house and knocked on the door. Judging by the way the light was falling through the trees, it was just about dinner time.

"Hey guys," she grinned when she opened the door. "Need something to eat?"

Barbara was so nice it almost made me feel like crying. Her pretty gold hair looked soft on her shoulders, and she looked put-together, with pink blush on her cheeks and a charm bracelet on her slender wrist. I noticed a bumblebee charm, a ladybug charm, and a butterfly, all silver. Pretty things owned by other people.

"Yeah," Matthew said, stepping past her into the house.

We sat at Barbara's kitchen table with its plastic gingham tablecloth and ate chicken nuggets with ketchup, plus two tall glasses of milk. This seemed very fine dining to me. She didn't even have any kids, so I knew she kept foods like this in the freezer just for Matthew and me—for the afternoons when we knocked on her door, probably looking very neglected and pitiful.

Barbara was in her early 20s. Her husband was friendly and kind, and they had a pretty house. I assumed they were rich—their life looked perfect. I had no idea her husband was abusing her. Lying in the dark in her spare bedroom that night, I held onto the broken angel and cried.

CHAPTER 6

It was the same nightmare as usual. The one from Hellraiser.

I ran as fast as I could from that monster. I didn't even have to look at him to know who it was. The monster with the pins in his face. I ran so I couldn't feel my legs and couldn't feel my lungs. Like usual, part of me knew it wasn't real. Knew it was just a dream. But I knew just the same, sure as anything, that I had to get away. Fear is resilient, doesn't need the caveat of reality to feel real.

"Kids—KIDS!"

I jolted awake, but my uneasiness didn't fade. The source of anxiety was only shifted onto the waking plane. My body tensed out of the warm lull of sleep.

"Better hurry," Matthew mumbled as he shuffled past my bedroom.

In the living room, Mom stood pointing at the carpet, hair all shagged out like a clearance-rack Medusa.

"You two clean this," she said plainly.

I was still mostly asleep, but it was clear to me that she was still drunk from the night before, her eyes bleary and unfocused, figure swaying in the morning sun. At her feet, the carpet was wet like something spilled. I could smell urine and beer.

"Oh my god, clean your puke? No fucking way!" Matthew shouted in disgust, backing away.

I looked at the soiled floor. I looked at Mom, in her stained tank top and denim shorts. Her legs were two thin crags of bruises and scabs, her arms slightly trembling as the hour of prime intoxication withdrew from the morning. Her face bloomed a rote hatred. Angry now. A familiar kind of angry.

"We got school," I said.

Her hand struck my face so fast I staggered back. Even stupid with booze, she was fierce.

"I am not cleaning your puke," Matthew repeated, reaching for his backpack.

Without words, Mom beat him casually, and he accepted it without much reaction. Let it run its course. I wondered how badly her blows really hurt him. She was powerful, but for me, the physical pain had mostly become meaningless. The vague outline of sensation on my skin. I had reached my saturation point in that kind of victimhood, where the stinging expires from the body. The real hurt happened deep inside. An industrious, vagrant pain.

"Clean!"

With dish soap and old sponges, Matthew and I knelt in the living room and scrubbed while Mom went to her room. The smell of Marlboros leaked out from under her door. It mutated with the odor of the puke pile and shocked the rest of sleep right out of me.

"Fuck this," Matthew muttered all the while.

I kept quiet for fear of him stomping off and forcing me to do the job on my own. I turned my head and gagged every so often—couldn't help it. It was more noxious than anything the twins ever expelled. My sponge ground soft, half-digested food into the fibers of the carpet. Froot Loops, clear as day, disintegrating in gold beer. Soggy vestiges of whatever scarcity was left within her.

We finished before long, but Mom still wouldn't let us go to school. I guess she thought we'd tell on her. Matthew might have—but I wouldn't. Never. The same appalling faith that he invested in our father, I invested in her. Our diametric hopefulness complemented each other, as did our incredible disappointment. Every time Mom pulled a stunt like this, I couldn't help but to compare it against a sweet memory, like the handful of times she played with me in the yard or the few semi-child-appropriate movies we watched together. The maintenance of the sanctity of her image was the most crucial duty of my life. Of course, I didn't realize what I was doing, or why it felt so draining. To be her daughter was to never stop moving, to hurriedly throw myself inside the goal-posts before she upended them once again.

I loved going to school, but we got in trouble for truancy because of how much she kept us home. We were her prisoners. To keep us out of her way or satisfy some sadistic urge within her, she would make us wash particularly filthy, obscure corners of the house—beneath the moldy pipes of the sink or by the crawlspace in the basement, scrape the deep intestine of the shower drain or soap the maggoty corners of the garage. Sometimes she would smash her empty liquor bottle against the kitchen table or front door during some manic episode, and wouldn't stop repeating an arbitrary phrase or word until we had swept every piece up.

There were worse punishments than staying home from school. If Mom was really mad, she'd put a dot on the wall higher than me and make me stand at its level on tippy toes. I appeased myself by pretending I was the ballerina in the music box I once saw at a toy store. I'd begged Mom for it, but she only thrashed my hands off her arm when I tried to speak to her, ignoring me completely. I had been enthralled with the ballerina the way I was with my dollar store angel, another embodiment of the impossible purity that seemed to exist nowhere in reality. But I could pretend. I could fill in the opposite space of Mom's indifference. If I got down off my toes she'd stroll over and strike me. It hurt my feet, but I always got over it.

Always.

Still, Mom took most of her violence out on Matthew. If anything reminded her of a person she didn't like, she hated it passionately—a song, a kid, a dog—anything. It didn't matter if it made sense. It didn't matter if it was fair. Despite the swimming of her sloppy logic, there were always a few hot targets. Matthew reminded Mom of Bob, so he got beat. It was really that simple. He was irrevocably guilty just for looking like his father.

I heard a car door close and looked up from my science project. Aunt Renee was trudging up the driveway, enormous black leather purse strapped across her body. Grown women always seemed to have top security clearance for throwing mysterious objects in those ambulant little black holes. I wanted one of my own, to squirrel away mythical treasures into, maybe a clipboard to make it official. I threw down my materials and rushed into the living room as the door swung open. Some new energy to stir the air, to fill the blank page of the day with the unknowable operations of adulthood.

"Hi!"

"Hey, Emma! Whatcha doing?" Aunt Renee came over to check on us often—she only lived 10 minutes away.

"Stupid science project," I answered.

"Matthew, get over here," she called, waving her hand. He begrudgingly abandoned the television to stand before Aunt Renee. She grabbed him by the shoulders and lined us up side by side, eyeing us thoroughly. She crossed her big arms across her bosom and pursed her lips.

"Okay, Matthew. What's up? How's your mom treating you guys?"

"Like shit."

"Has she been drinking?"

Behind Aunt Renee, Mom waved her hands frantically. *No,* she mouthed, shaking her head violently.

"Yes," he said.

Aunt Renee turned to me. "Emma? How's she been treating you?"

Mom widened her eyes at me. It was impossible to refuse the law of that gaze.

"Good," I lied.

Mom knew Aunt Renee would tell their parents about anything dangerous going on. That would lead to some static interference of the family that could expel her forever from me. The contingency of her presence always dangled above my consciousness, put the fear right in me. I still wanted to be with my mother. I still wanted to actualize the way she *could* be. So I protected her. Hoped she'd be proud of me. Maybe I'd get a hug in recompense.

When Aunt Renee left, Mom beat Matthew.

But not me.

Aunt Renee knew Mom was a drunk and delusional. Sometimes she thought she'd fed us, but actually hadn't. She knocked pictures down, leaving broken glass on the floor that I'd find stuck in the soles of my feet like little splinters days later. A shining mixture of varying specks of sharp pain. They would work themselves to the surface eventually. Mom was always too numbed out to feel anything. She slashed herself up a few times during her rages, and the blood would drip from her knuckles or forearm like a blatant river disguised from her senses. She'd find blood stains the day after and accuse me or Matthew of some nonsense while her new wounds festered and scabbed up.

Deep down, Aunt Renee knew the danger we were truly in. Still, she never reported Mom. I don't know why. What I do know is that Aunt Renee had always wanted a daughter. She told me more than once that if Mom ever lost custody, which seemed likely at times, she wanted to keep me. And Aunt Renee would fight for us one day—but the court would decide in Dad's favor.

One day Matthew was sitting on a barstool in the kitchen eating a bowl of cereal, basking in the afterglow of spending a few days at Dad's house. He must have gotten a real jam-packed session of lewd girlie-talk now that he was approaching fourteen. His expression flickered over a spoonful of milk.

"I miss Dad," he grumbled.

I nodded like I understood, though I didn't. I'd rather have lived with Mom than Dad any day. I saw no appeal in orbiting his salacious actions, or brusque gruffness. There was no malleability to him the way there was sometimes with Mom. No ounce of tenderness to scrounge out. I did not share the coincidence of his maleness, could not reflect his image.

Mom approached Matthew from behind and punched him in the side of the head in one swift, easy blow. He toppled off the barstool and landed on the floor, though Mom was only 100 pounds. The bowl had fallen, and milk ran off the counter and onto the floor. Some of it sopped around his ankles, a failed osmosis.

"You little shithead," Mom snapped, kicking him over and over. I heard her kick the ripe air out of him, the floundering of his lungs. Action and reaction of her furious legs and the lurching of his breath. I saw him lying in the fetal position screaming his throat raw, and took off running. The screen door banged closed behind me. I don't remember where I went. But I had to get out of there.

I used to think Mom liked Matthew better than me since she always let him go play outside with his friends but made me stay home. But the truth was that she just wanted him away from her. Anything to send his familiar face into a far abyss, that spoiling reminder of our father. In the summertime, she'd let Dad have him for longer than the allotted 45 days, like a trinket re-gifted. Or she'd send him to camp. Anything to be rid of him.

When I came back home that night, Matthew was in his room with the door closed, and the house was silent. It was a silence gravid with the aftermath of violence and dejection. Its weight was commanding and widespread, a disparate anchor dispersed all about the dead house. I went into my own room and absently flipped through a book, wondering what Matthew was doing, if he was still crying. I felt for him. To witness my older brother in such a state was disturbing, despite his bullying. He still shared my blood, shared the consequences of Mom's tyranny. The image of him helpless on the floor would not leave my mind. It never would.

Matthew and I didn't talk about any of this stuff. We were disconnected emotionally from each other—and from everyone. Before I could even speak, he hated me. I can hardly blame him—he, like me, was not immune to the complexes we inherited. He was simply fulfilling the prophecy gravely etched into our bloodline. Resentment was only a prerequisite, if anything. I was used to him shoving me down the stairs and running me over with his bike. His cruel jokes and belittling language were but a natural consequence of Mom's lifestyle.

But this was nothing compared to what was to come—when he would take to using weapons, and the bruising would become impossible to hide. Another branch of the family tree had collapsed beneath the root's infection.

CHAPTER 7

Squeals of delight bubbled out of Mom's bedroom. I knew that sound—it was the twins, and they were into something. At two years old, wreaking havoc was their favorite pastime. They were carrying the inevitable torch of mischief that Matthew and I had lighted many years ago. Eager to see the damage, I peeked into the bedroom.

Varying shades of shimmery pinks and rich reds adorned the twins, the walls, the door—everything. They slapped at the ruined carpet, pleased with their work. The scent of nail polish was overwhelming, could have revived a corpse from recent death.

"Mom!" I called through laughter. "Come see!"

"Are you shitting me!" she screamed when she entered, which only made me laugh harder. I knew she wouldn't hurt the twins—otherwise I'd never have let her find out.

Looking back as an adult, I realize she must have left them alone for a very long time. Kids can get into stuff fast, but the level of damage they'd done made it obvious they'd been in there for more than 20 minutes. What if they'd poured it in their eyes? What if they'd drank it?

But Mom didn't seem to worry much about that. She was very angry, however, that they'd painted the plastic, glow-in-the-dark skeleton that hung on the back of her door—a cheap Halloween decoration. But something she valued.

These chintzy odd composites of useless capital, all somehow conducive to her self-image. How many pieces of these little nothings to create *something*?

The twins' blue eyes sparkled as Mom's went hard like stones. Crags of dust and weariness. Murky. It was like witnessing an over-wired robot resetting its circuits. Like a low gravity on the edge of a ghastly tipping point. It was often preceded by some sort of paroxysm, but this time she was only silent, glassy.

She would never clean that carpet—didn't even bother trying. Eventually it turned into a shell of dry gore. Nothing she wasn't used to.

Holidays and birthdays were special to Mom. Birthdays were full of games and presents. A few times a year these small beacons would emerge from the dry waters—something to cherish, a reason to be in awe. For Halloween she stuffed huge pumpkin trash bags full of leaves. The front yard was adorned with hay bales and scarecrows. Bats hung from the ceiling and spiderwebs were strung in every corner. The dark matrix of Mom's psyche manifested into something strangely beautiful.

Mom thought the more objects she provided, the more she was showing us love. In a way, it worked. I was always so excited for holidays, especially Christmas. The doorways were framed in Christmas cards. Little ceramic villages occupied tables. Lights twinkled on the roof. A train chugged around the tree. Mom left dust on the floor to mark the footsteps of Santa and his reindeer. She did this all to make herself feel good, though I do think she got some joy from seeing us happy too.

Christmas was always at Aunt Renee's or Grandma's, and we'd load up 15 dishes of food to bring. It was so exciting. This was something, at least—right? There was some semblance of meaning that we could rally blindly behind, some scarcity pockets of purpose. This was some kind of life, with at least two days to look forward to every year. Better than living with Dad. He never even had a Christmas tree. There was no medium that linked us, since I had a ways to go before reaching the legal age of shameless debauchery.

"Did you see what the twins did?" I giggled, shuffling into Matthew's room.

He turned to me sharply, and I flinched, braced for a punch or a smack. But instead he yanked me by the arm, forced me up the ladder to his top bunk bed.

"What do you want?" I grumbled, obeying to prevent injury. He never let me share his space, let alone his own bed. Some sense in me immediately sank. Something was different.

"Shut up," he mumbled. He climbed on top of me and pushed down hard with his body.

"What are you doing?" I whined, wiggling underneath him.

"Shut up!" His face was red and contracted above mine. This wasn't the same physical harshness I was used to. Quick drags of violence were well a part of my vocabulary, but the steady constant of his pressing somehow felt more violating, more personal.

After a little while he stopped, and I ran to my room. I was confused—if he wanted to hurt me, why not just punch me or kick me like he usually did? Why the sudden diversion from his usual brusqueness? It pitted a denseness in my gut, made me lower my head.

I was embarrassed. I didn't know it was necessarily wrong, but I knew it was something not to talk about. When I was older I spoke to Matthew about it. That's when we started having physical fights. He backed off then, so I thought he got the message—but I learned he was just touching my sister instead. He was fourteen. She was six.

One night Mom was passed out cold during a movie. She looked to be tucked safely in her nightly air of oblivion. Matthew knew perfectly well that it would take a meteor shower to wake her up in her drunken state. He climbed on top of her and touched her breasts and went into her underwear—something he probably would have gotten away with if she hadn't miraculously woken up.

I kept quiet—pretended not to witness the whole scene. But of course, it was just one more trauma I'd never forget.

They've been under the same roof fewer than ten times since that day.

CHAPTER 8

Everyone remembers September 11, 2001.

I was in fourth grade. I was walking home from school when Aunt Renee pulled up alongside me.

"I'll take you home, Emma," she called through the open window.

It was nice outside—sunny—but I got in the car. William was there too, headphones on.

"Emma, your mom is really sick."

I buckled in. "Is she barfing?" I cringed from the thought of having to sponge up her puke again.

Aunt Renee sighed. I couldn't see her from the backseat, but I could feel her tension. The air was paretic and heavy, held some sour intimation. My muscles stiffened.

What Aunt Renee wouldn't tell me that day was that while all four of her kids were at school, Mom had taken a bottle and a half of pills and waited to die.

At her house, Aunt Renee sat me at the table and gave me a peanut butter sandwich.

"Actually, two things happened today," she said. "Your mom got sick, and something else happened too." She looked down. "There was a plane crash."

I ate the sandwich, rubbing the substance against my fingers. It reminded me of puppy chow. "Where at?"

William was in the other room, the TV tuned to monster trucks, punctuating our fragile conversation with abrupt rallies of support for his favorite wheels. I guess he'd already been told and was now onto more important endeavors. The trucks zoomed and smashed in the background while Aunt Renee's face hung defeated before me.

"New York."

"Cool."

She shook her head. "It wasn't an accident—it was an attack. A lot of people died."

I looked up. "Like the whole plane?" She nodded, her hand pressed against her cheek.

"Thousands of people."

Thousands? Was that normal for a plane crash? It was impossible to envision that sweltering number, and the respective terror endured by each of them. I could hardly bear the magnitude of my class size, let alone a number stuffed with ciphers. Oh well. I wouldn't concern myself with the events of that day until I saw the news coverage days later —the replays of the planes slicing into the buildings, which I had assumed to be indestructible. The footage of the towers crumbling all the way down into dust. The discord of human sound before and after death. The bleating faces in their hysterical emergence from the clouds of ash.

The people jumping.

The two tragedies of that day seemed to me somehow intertwined. One and the same. Like maybe if the towers hadn't fallen, Mom wouldn't have taken the pills. Maybe if Mom hadn't taken the pills, the towers wouldn't have fallen. It didn't make sense, but I felt it with a great sense of conviction. It was a degenerate causal loop that ate me up at night when I tried to sleep. But there was no way to reconcile those two tragedies, no way to make sense of the disparate mosaic of our lives. Another precious thing is shattered, and more blood is drawn in gathering the pieces.

All four of us would have to stay at Aunt Renee's house for a while until Mom got better. It was nice to have a respite from the turbulence of living beneath her shadow, but the longing for her never left me. I fell asleep imagining her face—pale and joyous—trying to meter out where in recovery she was. How long it would be until I could be beside her and hear her voice.

She didn't call, and we didn't visit. I wondered if she even knew about those planes. Those people. People like her, to whom fate resigned a bitter hand. Smote by circumstance. But she still had a chance at life.

I wondered if she'd even care.

"Did you know Mom wants to kill us?"

I looked down at Ava, her curly ponytail lopsided and sagging. She was six years old and told all kinds of bizarre stories. Her tales were equivalent in intensity to Dad's sexual escapades, but instead centered on her heroic ventures into the neighbor's yard or Mom's bedside drawers.

"Just you," I teased, shrugging.

Ava looked horrified, spilled white with the realization of one's own mortality. Her adolescent face turned wise in an instant. She turned and bolted out the front door.

"Where's she off to?" Tim asked as he emerged from Mom's room, kneading his hair. He looked irritated, jumpy.

Again I shrugged. I didn't much care for Tim. He was nice enough on the surface, but like most of her boyfriends, something about him made me uncomfortable. There was some common denominator that bonded them all into one sordid, slopping figure. I avoided making eye contact. It always somehow felt safer that way. Like some peripheral image I could blink away.

"Well you stay here," he said, shifting his weight. Agitated. Nervous.

I sat down on the couch, oblivious. No idea that this was the last day Mom would ever have all her kids under the same roof.

"She's what!" Mom shrieked. I was unfazed—Mom screamed a lot. It was always best to stay somber during her episodes, to wait for the chaos to pass. Better than ending up the most convenient target near her.

Tim was whispering. Rubbing the back of his neck. Twitching, about to take stock of the panorama surrounding him.

"You do it your fucking self then!" and Mom stomped off. Nothing new. I focused on the drone of the TV. The white noise of her hysterics always eventually faded out. It was a simple war of attrition with her.

"Come on," Tim said. "We're going to the river."

"Why?"

He dragged me by the wrist past the bathroom, where I spotted Mom crouched on the floor. Sobbing.

"Gonna play hide and seek." He quickened his pace toward the door, clenching his grip.

Matthew followed us obediently, dragging Elijah along. "At the river?"

"What about Ava?" I asked as he led us out the back door, turning my head back. "And why's Mom crying?"

"Enough with the questions."

Outside, rain fell in cold, heavy drops. Sporadic. Without any rhyme or reason. A bestiary of bitter wetness and the futile gray of sky.

From inside, Mom wailed and screamed. *"My babies!"*

"What's she saying?"

But Tim just continued to lead us towards the woods, towards the river. Past the furious dew quickly gathering in our footsteps, the brush of branches that scraped against our legs. Further from the only polestar we had ever known, the only harbor. Soon her screams began to fade, upended by the sound of our clunky movement. And we just continued to follow.

The storm intensified rapidly, lightning splitting through the clouds. An omen. The air was febrile and prophetic, striking down on sour strips of space. Elijah screamed, rain splintering from his lashes.

In the distance, sirens wailed. People in police uniforms stormed toward the house. It was the only sound that outmatched the anguish of Mom. It sounded like our bang-snaps, but much more salient. Matthew and I ran back the way we came, the dreary gloss of flickering lights and serious men inflating in vision until we reached her. She did not look quite the same.

Mascara tears dripped down Mom's face, her eyes wide and red and insane as she was ushered into the cruiser with her hands behind her back. The cold caul of glass shuttered across her expression, reflecting the mockery of color that alighted her face. The perfection of the American dream sweltering upon her screaming: red and blue, red and blue.

"My babies!" she cried, walleyed and aghast, thrashing about. She looked truly desperate this time, tapping her forehead against the window. But it was hard to discern which myriad of personalities this claim was coming from.

I stood and watched her. Just watched, like a movie. I wondered what was going on. Why would the cops pick up Mom now? What was different this time? It was only another flare in the prolonged series of her moods. Mom looked at me briefly as she was crammed into the cruiser. But she didn't see me. Her eyes were shrouded with confusion. Two obsidian obelisks.

They loaded Tim up next. He said nothing, and he did not

look at us. It only seemed natural that he should accompany her, wherever they were taking her. For once, I did not want to go with her. It was as if the portrait of her body had been possessed. She was not even equal with the mother that forced me to watch grisly torture scenes on the television. This time, the scene was real. She was the clamoring thing to behold in awe and terror being dragged away by outside forces.

Someone wrapped a blanket around my shoulders. A temporary relief against the sodden sky. "Your aunt is on her way. You're all gonna be okay. Hey, I like your dress."

I looked down at the pattern, indistinguishable to me. Red and blue flashed across the fabric, some distorted garish flag.

"What are those, sunflowers?"

CHAPTER 9

The plan had been simple. Tim would drown us kids in the river, shoot Mom in the head, then himself.

Running in her bare feet to a neighbor's house, Ava saved all our lives. She saved us from a fate of noxious newspaper headlines detailing the family of bloodless bodies found stewing around the river. 'Innocent Children Killed by Crazed Mother in Bloody Suicide Pact', 'How One Mother Prompted a Man to Kill her Family.' Perhaps we would have been found by a fisherman or a child. Perhaps the town would have had vigils for us stuffed with emotional mothers who would say things like, "I can't believe a mother could do that to her children," or, "Those poor babies—they had their whole lives ahead of them." And then a few years later we would be just another expired tragedy blurred by time and more recent tragedies.

Though we narrowly escaped being drowned to death by a man we hardly knew, our resignation of fate was simply transferred into different hands. We were back living with our father.

Although my mother was sick, at least we got three meals a day under her roof (when she was present). We all had our own room. We were able to interact with other family members. We had toys. We had friends. Her emotional neglect paved space for us kids to be inventive and creative, even if that meant finding affection through neighbors like

Barbara. We had free reign to do as we pleased. Sometimes I could curl up next to Mom while she was zonked out in front of a movie. I could rest my head on her arm and feel a moment of peace. With Dad, we had nothing but the clothes on our backs.

Our first night at Dad's, I sat on the sofa, stiff with grime, with Elijah on one side of me and Ava on the other. We couldn't turn the television on because Dad was listening to his music. In fact, he was listening to it at full volume. Classic country, same as always. The trailer vibrated with sound, buzzing up the corners and counters with the lonesome calls of a country-boy freshly abandoned by his miniskirt wearing love interest. We stared ahead at the blank screen, our distorted reflections staring back.

Beyond the TV, Dad sat at the kitchen table shirtless. Matthew sat across from him, his mirror image, having removed his own shirt. Between puffs of cigarettes and swigs of cheap beer, Dad sang along badly, wiping his grubby hands on his denim shorts. Matthew drank a Coke, looking pleased as ever, the before-picture of decades of hard living. It was difficult for me to imagine how Dad may have looked in his youth. He was the belligerent sort of character that youth seemed somehow to altogether evade, as if time knew him no other way than he was now. Hard and angry and threatening.

This would be the routine. Every night he would sit there with his beer, like clockwork. Every hour more cigarette smoke to be dispelled into the air, dumped into our lungs. More sour beer to stain the carpet, to join in harmony the dog piss and spoiled food. He never came down from his warm tin of intoxication, eyes slugging like ghosts from one hour to the next. Head lulling, only snapping to transient lucidity to take another swig.

"Emma," he grumbled, "cook."

I frowned. "No way. I don't know how."

"You're a woman, ain't you? Cook!" He flicked his cigarette toward me, eyes raw and commanding.

He directed me to the freezer, where a box of premade lasagna sat on the shelf. I turned the box over and read the directions—preheat? *Vent?*

"I can't—"

He slammed his beer down on the table, making me jump. "Shut up already, you dumb bitch!"

My heart ached and suddenly, terribly, I missed my mom. I felt isolated and overwhelmed at the same time, stuck in some smothering limbo. In the living room, the twins both cried. They were scared—they'd never been alone with Dad before. Their red faces bloomed like boiled tomatoes. The din of misery rose in my ears, helplessness. Matthew slouched at the table, grinning. He could feel the power dynamic shifting.

When I burned the stupid lasagna, I braced for Dad to beat me—but he didn't. Instead, with fire in his eyes, he declared: "Alright. Shit on the shingles it is."

He stood up and pushed his chair in with a slam. I stood and watched as he dug into the fridge for every leftover that sat decaying on the shelves—mac and cheese, canned corn, fried chicken, barbeque sauce—it didn't matter. He threw it all in a big pot and turned the burner on.

"Mattie and me are going for Taco Bell. Y'all can enjoy your shit on the shingles when it's done."

A strange smell started to emit from the pot as they left. How would I know when it was done?

After some time had passed, I scooped some of the slop into three bowls. The twins and I sat at the table, trying not to gag as we took small bites of the stuff. Dad burst through the door, laughing hysterically, Matthew in tow. They held burritos in their hands. Matthew made sure to sit where I could see him. He smiled at me while I gagged over my bowl.

I can't eat leftovers to this day.

Sometimes we tried to throw the shit on the shingles away, enjoying Lays chips and mustard for dinner instead. But then Dad started checking the trash can, screaming that we were ungrateful.

As the twins got older and bigger, they needed more food. That's when Dad started accusing us of stealing his food, he drilled more locks on the fridge and pantry. Metal ones. We couldn't break them—we tried.

"The twins are hungry," I said weakly.

"Fat fucking pigs," Dad muttered drunkenly.

My new school was poor, and whites were the minority. I'd never even been in a classroom with someone of a different race, so when I was seated between two Mexican girls on my first day, it was a culture shock. I didn't fit in, and they knew it.

Us kids all struggled with our grades, especially Elijah. We didn't know at the time that he was autistic, and the teachers didn't notice or care, so he suffered more than the rest of us. Ava did all his homework for him so he could pass.

Soon it was time to bring Dad our report cards. I had assumed he wouldn't care, but he actually demanded that we give them to him—he even somehow knew when the end of the semester was, which amazed me.

I stacked mine on top, since it was the best, followed by Ava's, Matthew's, and Elijah's. Dad snatched them from my hand and spread them out on the table. I stepped back to escape his smell—cigarettes, beer and sweat.

"What the fuck?" he said. "You kids are really fucking idiots!"

Ava immediately started to cry, and she and Elijah sulked off to their rooms before Dad could get a look at them and decide to hit them. But Matthew and I didn't care about his screaming, and we didn't fear his blows. A vagrant kick or punch was part of the deal in living with him. He'd beat us for having the television volume too high, or for accidentally waking him up from his murky beer naps. The report cards only provided him a sufficient pretense to do to us what he was going to do anyway.

By the time the next report cards arrived, I had a plan. It was mostly out of concern for the twins that I contrived a way to temper his hostility. Ava especially had begun to fear the end of the semester. It was my job to protect her.

"C's are actually good," I informed Dad confidently as I gathered the twins' report cards. "As long as you're not below a D, it means you're doing fine. No one actually gets A's anymore—they kind of got rid of that."

He grabbed them and squinted at our grades, mostly C's and D's. He was hunched over shirtless in his favorite chair, smoking. Ten empty beer cans at his feet, leaking warm fluids from their metallic mouths. Clearly he'd been swimming for a while now. "Huh." He glanced up at his sidekick Matthew. "That true?"

He nodded.

Having quit school at just ten years old, Dad didn't know much better. "You're still a bunch of little slackers," he muttered, tossing the report cards aside and cracking open a fresh can. "Emma, clean this mess up." He kicked the cans out from below him and I quickly gathered them without protest. It didn't matter how much stronger he was than me, how much bigger or louder. I realized then I had something he did not. I realized the power in successfully deceiving. In making people believe whatever you wanted them to believe. I grinned—success.

Dad didn't come to our plays or other events, but I didn't mind. I would have been humiliated if my peers had seen him in his dirty shorts and known he was my dad. But he went to all Matthew's cross country meets. Did he really love him more, or did he just want to hurt us? As long as the twins and I were safe, I considered myself lucky. We mostly stayed in our room, waiting for morning to come so we could leave the house for school. I would read to them or make up silly stories to make them laugh, try my best to answer questions beginning to bud in their minds. Usually revolving around Mom, and where she was and what she was doing. Always my answer was the same—that she was getting better somewhere far away from here but that we would see her again soon.

"When is soon?" Ava would ask.

I could only ever respond by the same, "Soon."

When Dad was finally approved for food stamps, I was put in charge of the shopping, though of course I had no idea how. I wandered through Kroger, feeling very much like a child. Grown-ups looked at me curiously. I tried to peek into their shopping carts—what was I supposed to get? Lost, I reached for the foods I was used to—boxed mac and cheese and mashed potatoes, canned green beans and corn. It was all I knew, and I was scared to upset Dad. For years, this was all we ate. No one complained, and sometimes I felt like a real housewife.

One night, as we ate our mac and cheese, the phone rang. Dad grabbed it off the wall. "What!" he demanded. Then he went still, lowering his fork. "Oh, yes. Oh, of course, ma'am."

I knew right away who that was—Child Protective Services.

"They're comin' tomorrow," he said simply as he hung up the phone. "Y'all better wash those grubby faces and put on your smiles."

CPS came often to check in on us, but they always gave enough notice for Dad to stuff the house with pretzels and cookies and other delicious treats. It almost looked like a normal household for a couple of days. Then when they left, he'd eat it himself or throw it all away. Worse yet, he'd let it sit there until it rotted, forbidding us to go anywhere near it. We watched with grumbling stomachs each day as the food moldered into inedible fodder.

"Fat fuckers," he said, locking the fridge.

The next day, I sat on the couch trying to think of some sort of signal I could give the CPS lady when she arrived. Something to let her know we weren't okay. To let her know we were hungry. Hurting. Tired.

It was February, and for the first time all winter, Dad turned the heater on. I was almost comfortable. He never ran the AC during the summers—I often woke up in a puddle of sweat, my hair slicked to my neck and my legs stuck together. We had to open our windows just to breathe, but the screens were damaged so bugs would get through—then we were hot and spotted with itchy bug bites. Every morning I'd awake to peel the pocks of half-dead squirming things off me. He said it was due to money—but he always had money for beer and cigarettes. A 24 pack every night, to be exact.

When the knock at the door came, Dad sprung up from his place at the kitchen table and glared at us all sharply. "Don't fuck up," he hissed. The place was moderately clean thanks to the hours Ava and I spent scrubbing every surface and throwing out the ash-puddles of cigarette butts while Dad sat there sipping and smoking. The piss scent was still there, though. That was unavoidable.

I faced the blank TV, but I could hear him greeting the CPS

lady. It was usually the same one, Deborah, with her tacky smile and her purple plastic clipboard. I wondered what she wrote on there. Her eyes would loom up from her tilted skull as she scribbled anonymous notes, extracting vague splotches of information of other people's lives. There was a strange intimacy in these evaluations. Here was the platonic eye of an assimilated woman, the unity of the healthy and responsible world, scanning the daily landscape of our lives for some semblance of love.

"Hi kiddos," she grinned as she entered, her flat brown shoes sticking to the linoleum. "How's it going?" It seemed to me all these sane, well-formed women I'd seen in waiting rooms or grocery stores were the same person. They had the same floral perfumes, the same bright shades of lipstick, the same hairdresser and voice. They were always in the harrowing middle of some paramount project, ushering their children around to practices or asking questions with self-assurance. She was just another woman in the long list of women who were not my mother.

"Fine," Matthew said from the armchair.

"Me and Daddy are gonna be chatting in the kitchen for a little while, okay?"

Dad smiled hard at us. We nodded. My chest contracted as they walked down the hall. How was I supposed to get her attention now? There were levels of deception I was willing to indulge if I thought the reward was worth it. But the risk this time was too high. If I couldn't pull it off, the consequences would likely be upgraded to an entirely new level of terror.

In the kitchen, I heard Dad's voice, sweet as candy: "Gosh,

I'm just so grateful I got those poor kids away from their mother."

Dad woke up at four every morning, made coffee, then started on the beer. Each and every day, the same. Coffee, beer, classic country. Cussing and criticizing. Driving his family away. Always caught up in that hackneyed time loop.

He had healthcare, but he never used it for us. We never saw a doctor the entire time we were with him. Ava and Elijah saw a dentist once, only because I took them. We had to learn how to walk it off, to clean it up and bandage it ourselves—whatever pain it was we were dealing with. I'm pretty sure there were some fractured bones in the mix, but nothing severe enough to stir him to any kind of alertness. I had to grow up very quickly—though in many ways, I was stunted. The more energy I expended on the futile task of maintaining some notion of safety, the more drained I became. Hollow. There was a vacant lot within me that could not be filled by anything. Some things just never heal quite right.

While I was cooking, shopping, and caring for the twins, Dad and Matthew were buying trashy cars and rigging them to run—sort of. For hours, dead engines painfully revved to screeching half-life until they found it satisfactory enough to sell. It only added a new layer of pungency to the air. Smog that traveled from my father's mind to the lungs of his wretched children.

They made huge profits this way, and they quickly started to fight about money. Suddenly there was another option in the endless rotunda of things to get pissed off about.

"I'm doing as much work as you," Matthew barked. He was quickly becoming Dad's double. There was a new urgency to his volatility, a new edge. "We should be splitting the cash!"

Dad laughed bitterly, nursing his beer in his usual spot. "Fuck off. You're just a kid, you don't have any expenses."

Matthew lunged, socking Dad in the jaw. Dad toppled from his chair, beer spilling across the floor. A retrofit image of Matthew wailing in the milk-sopped carpet as Mom stood over him. A cyclical harvest quickly plundered by the inheritance of abuse. Another son to stand and bloom.

"I need more cash!" Matthew shouted, standing over him.

Dad scrambled to his feet and tackled him. They had these intense fistfights often, eager to harm one another. Dad never closed-fist punched us other kids, but he loved to slap me and drag me by my hair. Women belonged in the kitchen, so if Ava or I ever tried to go outside, he took the opportunity to hit us. Other times we were doing nothing at all—he just wanted to hurt us. It gave him pleasure, I guess. A visible match to his cause agony. A mirror.

Dad was stronger than Mom, but somehow his abuse didn't hurt nearly as much. There was no pretense of love he was betraying by beating us. There wasn't much of anything in him. Each triple-blow felt like nothing, nothing, nothing.

CHAPTER 10

The hearing was set for Tuesday.

I wore my best clothes—a blue polo that used to belong to Matthew, and jeans that were so small I couldn't button them. I tied the front closed with dental floss. I had to represent Mom well—this would decide her fate, and mine too. I imagined she was just as anxious as me, just as eager to be reunited.

I was ecstatic at the idea of leaving Dad's. I was old enough to decide who I wanted, and I wanted Mom. I pictured our future lives through the rose-colored lenses a daughter decidedly wears for her mother. She was the apex of my ellipse, even when apart from her. My mind never left her. There was a self-renewing source of faith within me that could never be diminished, no matter what she did. Even if Dad had treated me well, I'd still have chosen my mom, and he knew that. So he hired a good lawyer. Money couldn't buy us new clothes or better food, but it could buy a sober old man in loose suits that smelled of mothballs.

"He'll get better if we stay with him," Matthew insisted. "He just wants us to stay."

I rolled my eyes. "Don't listen to him," I whispered to the twins. We knew Dad was evil. The division in the house had been evident from the beginning, and the twins and I were always on the wrong side of it.

My grandparents and Aunt Renee spent thousands of dollars trying to get us back home because they knew what type of man Dad was. But it was a tough battle. I didn't understand why it couldn't be simpler. We were the ones living this every day, facing this abuse. Shouldn't we be the ones who decide where we rest our heads at night? Shouldn't we get some say in our constant reality?

I hated my new life. I hated shit on the shingles and I hated classic country. I hated being locked inside all day, lonely and lost. I hated waking up and still being in the greasy trailer. Every day I hated everything. Mostly, I hated Dad.

Waiting outside the courtroom, I was restless. I paced anxiously between the twins, who swung their legs over the linoleum. The hall was very quiet and very musty. Distant shoe soles clanked from polar ends of the hallway, echoing into silence. My heart fluttered as I brooded over exactly what I was going to say; how I was going to say it. Matthew just sat shaking his head, cussing under his breath. His dark hair covered his eyes as he looked toward the floor.

After minutes or maybe even hours, Dad and his lawyer came out.

"I'm ready," I said, stepping forward. "I'm ready to talk to the judge."

"You won't need to testify," the lawyer announced proudly. He was a skinny man whose suit didn't fit right. It looked like it came from a prom shop. "You're all going to stay with your father."

I looked up at Dad, who smiled to expose his yellow teeth. He looked like an animated skull, sardonic and smug. Through the open door of the courtroom, I saw Mom and Grandma and Grandpa standing from their seats and lunged forward. There they were, fresh within my line of vision after endless months staring at piss stains on the rug.

"Eh!" Dad grabbed my arm hard and held me back.

Tears welled hotly in my eyes. My sternum quivered as if to open. I felt desperate.

"Mom!" I called, my throat constricting around the word. Dad's hand burned my arm like an iron off the fire, a paternal Indian burn. "Let me go see her," I sobbed. Her image bubbled and bleached out as my tears displaced her. It seemed everything I did only tore her further away from me.

My crying made Ava cry too. Dad grabbed her in his other hand and hauled us away.

"We're going home," he said. I looked back until my three beacons of safety were yanked out of vision by the shadow of the hallway. I felt delicate and raw, like an assistant in the proximity of a murdered prophet.

Years later I would learn that Mom had been caught drinking and driving a couple of weeks before the hearing, ruining any chance she had to get us back.

She didn't want us.

Dad didn't want us, either, though—he just wanted to win.

One of the only positive things in my life for a while was my horse Lenna. Dad bought her for me after the hearing. Whether he actually wanted to bring me some happiness, or he just wanted me to shut up, I didn't know. But it worked. For three months, I loved that horse more than I loved anything. She was my best friend. My only companion. My solace.

"Hey, let me ride it," Matthew demanded one afternoon, grabbing her reins.

I stroked Lenna's long brown nose. "Not a chance."

"Come on." He shoved me away easily, grabbing hold of the horse and hoisting himself up clumsily.

"Matthew, she doesn't know you!"

He kicked her roughly, and she startled, running awkwardly. I cringed at the sight of it, tense for whatever antics he might try to pull. It seemed every day he only became more and more impetuous.

"Yee-haw!" Matthew shrieked with pride, galloping further away from me.

As they neared a fence, Lenna bucked swiftly, launching him off and directly onto a cactus. I smiled. "Good Lenna." My own little warrior to love and defend me. I felt special for that, knowing that she accepted me and refused him.

"Fucking bitch horse!" he whined, carefully extracting himself from the spiny cactus. Little spokes stuck out from his arms and torso like a medieval painting. Flaking spots of blood that I made fun of him for, chicken-pox and cooties. I imagined all the times he ate Taco Bell while I fumbled around with a couple of rancid noodles, and laughed.

Lenna was used to abuse from Matthew and Dad. Dad had some "horse trainer" come out and try to break Lenna of her bad habits early on. But she was rather stubborn, moored only to her wild instincts. She was beautiful in her naturalness, free in a way I could never be. She seemed at one with herself, perfectly attuned to some other reality as she wandered the yard and flicked her ears and grazed the grass. Dad and the trainer took turns beating the poor animal with a metal bucket while she bucked and neighed. I screamed until my throat was raw, but it didn't matter. It was only the sound of another live animal in aguish.

On my 13th birthday, Dad sold Lenna. I was relieved to have her safe from the abuse, so I didn't fight it too much—but it wrecked me. He even dragged me along to the meetup so I could witness her being taken away. I sobbed deeply as the sale took place. My safe-stash of joy was now outed, completely depleted. The tremoring within my empty ribs would not stop, and my chest felt concave.

"It's a bitch horse," Matthew said, as if to comfort me.

Sick with the loss, I sprang forward and kicked the man who was leading Lenna away—her new owner.

"Hey!"

"Emma you little fucker—" Dad set off after me, and I ran like hell all the way to the car, where I sat in the back seat and cried for Lenna and for everything else I'd lost. I had no toys, no family, no home. Nothing that belonged to me. No one that cared about me. I was utterly empty, full of nothings. A vacuum.

"You know," Dad said on the drive home, "it wasn't your animal anyway."

"He bought it for *me*," Matthew chimed, turning his head back to smile at me. "But it was a bitch, so we gave it to you."

Dad chuckled in agreement. My heart swelled and contracted rhythmically, the tides of my pain endless. Something treacherous within me was building up, some degenerate actualization. My saturation point was approaching. I could feel it in the sickly syrup heaviness of my bones. It was too much to even raise my head to look out the window.

Dad loved to give and take away. It was a concept I grew to know very well. He would find out what I really wanted, string me along, then break it, sell it, or do whatever he had to do to take it away from me. The same perverse sequence each time, all for the grand climax of witnessing the spinning wheel of my sorrow. Each time this happened, I felt myself split in two. One part of me slowly calcified into an apathetic aegis. The other part slowly wilted by some chemical reaction.

The living part of me was attached to animals. I used to bring stray dogs home and hide them in my room, giving them my food. Giving them life and affection. Unlike my parents, I could not continue to beat a whimpering thing, or to starve a skeletal stomach. I'd make warm beds for them beside my own made from soiled blankets and piles of dirty clothes. Wake up just to pet them, to assure them that they were not alone. Someone was watching out for them. I did this dozens of times. For however brief a time, it gave me a sense of purpose. A hint of love.

"You can keep this one," Dad would say. "But you're in charge of it. I don't wanna see no piles of shit around, either."

For some reason, I believed him every time. Desperation, I guess. My heart would fill up with something like love. Then I'd go off to school, and when I came home the dog would be gone. Loss after loss after loss. A perpetual excavation of what I loved and who I was.

Nothing pleased him more.

I felt isolated no matter where I was. At school I tried to be invisible, humiliated by my hand-me-down clothes and dirty hair. I was ashamed just to exist. At home I hid in my room and tried not to interact with anyone. Neither place was better than the other—both brought their own pains and their own standard of deportment, which was mostly just keeping my mouth shut and not making eye contact with anyone. Each day was an indistinguishable blur of darkness; a bleak mix of misfortunes and depressions. A wasteland. I struggled to find something to hold onto.

I was failing science, and I had to go to tutoring early each morning. My teacher turned to me one morning, his face twisted up in disgust. "Do you smoke?"

I recoiled, shrinking into my seat. "No."

"Well." He scrunched his nose and turned away. "That's interesting."

After this, I was always conscious of how close I sat to

people, terrified to offend them with my smell. The smell of stale cigarette smoke, of spilled beer, of an old shirt not washed in weeks.

The smell of poverty.

CHAPTER 11

At 13, I learned I could make money by cutting grass in the neighborhood with Matthew. Of course, he used the job as another opportunity to torment me. He got me to do all the work, didn't pay me, *and* he got to irritate me. Some would call that a hat trick.

"Hey Emma," Matthew called. Pushing the lawnmower, I turned toward him. He was standing near some shrubbery holding the weed eater. My heart lurched. I had developed a crippling fear of weed eaters because of him. His brows were furrowed, smile scathing.

Laughing, he turned it on and thrust it into the rocks, flinging them up at me. I ran as sharp rocks struck the backs of my legs and head. I felt blood dripping hotly into my socks. I felt myself being cut open and exposed, and the indifference my lost flesh would suffer as it simmered and dried out on the pavement. Little bits of blood to step around.

To this day, I won't go anywhere near a weed eater that's running. It's pathetic—just one more childhood scar. Another memory in which to trap my future.

It was late at night, and Laura and I were sitting across from one another on my bedroom floor dipping hot Cheetos in margarita salt—a delicacy.

"You seriously had sex with him?" I whispered, giggling.

I was 13, and Laura was 15—she'd been held back two years. She was my best friend, and we were always together.

"Yeah," she shrugged, licking the coarse salt from her lips. "It was okay."

I was amazed. Though I'd been exposed to sex very young, the idea of my peers participating in the act was astounding. It was as if they carried some Prometheus of wisdom inside them for having simply done the act. Their coolness while they slung their backpacks over their shoulders. The uninspired acquisition of such an exclusively adult ritual. How could they act so natural about something that seemed so unnatural? Would I do that one day too?

Laura's mom was in prison, and she lived with her grandpa two blocks over from me. Our bond came not so much from a conscious comparison of our family lives, but from the byproduct of what such dynamics do to young personalities. Our troubles attracted us to each other.

"That looks good on you," she added, nodding toward me. I looked down at my outfit—the shirt was hers, *Hollister* printed across the chest. Laura was more than six feet tall and very skinny, but I somehow managed to fit into her clothes. Her grandpa bought her expensive name brand clothing—things I'd never seen before. She even taught me to straighten my hair with a pillow and an iron.

When I discovered conditioner, I thought I had to leave it in all night. My hair looked like butter the next day, but I didn't know any better. She took me under her wing—I needed her.

"Thanks," I said, smiling. She was the only one who ever complimented me on how I looked. The model of feminine confidence that I tried to assume.

"Hey, I've got a game." She put the bag of Cheetos down on the carpet. "It's really fun, I made it up a couple years ago."

"Let's play," I said, leaning forward eagerly.

"Okay." Laura moved forward and placed her hands around my neck, which made me laugh.

"The game is you kill me?"

She smiled, her fingers tightening around my throat. I felt my pulse begin to hammer in my eyes.

"We do it 'til you black out."

I kept laughing, but it was getting hard to suck in any air and the pressure kept tightening around my skull. My eyes felt ready to pop. Static wheels of blackness began to tumble around my vision, closing in on me. And then I guess I did black out, Laura's smiling face wavering above me momentarily, and then gone.

I woke up with a jolt, immediately panicked.

"It's okay, honey," an unfamiliar voice said.

"Where am I?"

"You're in an ambulance. We're going to the hospital."

I looked around, but there was only this lady and a bunch of strange equipment. My body bounced on the bumpy road. The white interior and gleaming metals felt confronting. Where was Laura? How long had I been out? My head swelled and receded like a ticking clock.

"Have you ever had a seizure before, Emma?"

I felt dizzy. "Where's Dad?"

"Your dad couldn't come. But you're safe."

I spent the night at the hospital alone, dazed and confused. A flurry of immaculate-looking figures in white wafted in and out of my room with various liquids and pills and needles. I couldn't stop shivering, though I wasn't particularly cold. I wondered how Mom would react if she knew her little girl was lying alone in a hospital bed. Of course, I already knew the answer.

When I went home the next day, Laura called and told me that I'd started to seize when she choked me, and I wouldn't wake up. So she called an ambulance and told Dad that I'd started to seize without explanation. He didn't question it.

He simply didn't care.

"Watch," Laura said. "Like this."

I sat on the sofa with a few people from school and watched Laura and her boyfriend James have sex on the rug. I was 13.

"Everyone does it," the boy next to me whispered.

James was 18. He and Laura were finished very quickly. It hadn't looked like much of anything to me. Fortunately, it was too dark to see the details, though the noises were revealing enough.

“Go ahead,” Laura smiled at me as she pulled her skirt down.

“I don’t know any of these guys,” I whispered, heart pounding. I could feel the dynamic in the room changing, the attention shifting. I could feel the eyes behind me analyzing me, storing my data into downloads to be later remembered. That creeping feeling of spotlight isolation began again, staking itself in my chest and fluttering like a caged animal.

She shrugged and pointed to the boy beside me. “How about him?”

Dad had never talked to me about sex, and I didn’t have my mom. It’s not like those years of watching her have sordid, sloppy encounters with random men anatomically enlightened me in any way. Something about the idea of fulfilling the act that my mother so often and recklessly indulged made my stomach feel sour. The only lesson I’d ever extracted from it was the depth and immediacy of men’s brutality.

I didn’t know much of anything—other than Laura said I was supposed to be having sex, just like grownups did. It barely made sense to me in theory. To blindly put it to practice was a truly petrifying idea. What was I supposed to do? Wouldn’t it hurt?

The guy next to me leaned over and kissed me then, and I kissed him back. He was James’ age. My stomach was sick —I knew I didn’t want to do this. But I knew I was going to. The lame thought flickered briefly through my head: I am becoming my mother. It seemed inevitable at that point to just let it happen.

After, I wanted my mom to feel pain for what she had done to me. I was doomed to this legacy, to repeat all her pointless mistakes and miseries because she was never there to map it out—not even a vague outline. I dialed her number hastily.

"I lost my virginity because of you!" I screamed into the phone. "I hate you!"

There was silence. Then, "Emma, I never wanted you to go through this." For a moment, my heart welled, and I hesitated, caught in my pain as if it were molasses. This brief window of affection I had envisioned in my hunger and sleeplessness. The anonymous words that a loving mother says to her daughter. The hook of her tenderness seized me, the softness of her words. Quickly I shook it off, calloused with betrayal. "Well, this is all you taught me," I snapped, hanging up.

We didn't talk for a long time after that.

CHAPTER 12

The twins and I approached Megan first. If she didn't pan out we'd try Jordan, and then Todd.

"Hi Megan," I said. "What are you doing after school?"

"Not driving you three to Dairy Queen again," she laughed. Megan was the nicest of our choices. And a push-over.

"Please," Elijah whimpered, something I'd taught him. Megan had a weakness for that sort of thing.

Not a lot of kids in Peachtree City had cars, but the ones who did, we frequently convinced to take us to Dairy Queen to see our grandparents. We had to choose people whose loyalties didn't lie with Dad—those who would keep our secret. By then we were quite decisive, judgements honed from years of being in survival mode.

Dad hated our grandparents. When Grandpa found out Dad was beating my mom when they were young, he banned him from his home. This—hoarding us kids away in his house—was Dad's revenge. But it only hurt us kids. His ego was far too precious to sacrifice for the livelihood of his family. None of us really knew each other by the time we were grown—this was all just time wasted. Time spent suffering to appease the drunk man's self-image.

Megan dropped the three of us off at Dairy Queen, where

Grandma and Grandpa were sitting at a table outside waiting for us. They were always in a good mood. Watching them smile and laugh was an instant contagion. We ran to them.

"Hello there," Grandma smiled, her hair white in the sun, reaching out to kiss our cheeks.

"Hi kiddos," Grandpa said, licking a vanilla ice cream cone. Their two ruddy, round faces side by side always alighted a feeling in me. A soaring lightness; a feeling of possibility. Or at least comfort.

I sat down across from them and smiled, waiting for them to ask me how my day was and what flavor I wanted. For a moment, I was happy.

Dad's brother Carl lived with us for a while. I don't know why—I didn't know why anything happened at Dad's house. This was just another surprise chapter in his series of dissipations.

Carl was a lot like Dad, only weaker—slower. Even dumber, maybe. He had the same sallow face and brutish mannerisms. And Dad treated him like shit, bossing him around and making fun of him every time he saw him. They only really got along when they were both piss-drunk to the point of being obnoxiously gregarious. Then it was all hunched-over cackling and vigorous cheers-ing that splashed up their warm beers into puddles.

One day I was in my room lying on the bed, a magazine held above my face. I blinked out absently at an image of a young woman in a tight black dress. The makeup on her face looked expensive. Her very skin looked expensive. She reminded me of the lady who auditioned Matthew for the commercial. Of the dreams I once had.

Carl came in and sat on my floor. He didn't say anything—he didn't even look at me. His empty eyes made my skin crawl. His breath lurched, curdled and bitter. I didn't like being around him. All I could think was that he murdered his mother, and that it probably was on purpose considering how oddly he always acted.

"Can I help you?" I snapped.

He shrugged, mumbling incoherent things. Then he reached up and touched my hip. I jerked away, heart suddenly beating in my chest.

"Are you drunk?"

But I knew he wasn't. He shrugged again, moving his hand to my inner thigh. My stomach flipped, and I froze. A blankness blanched my mind, a dead fear revived. Why couldn't I move? Why couldn't I kick him away? A mixture of fear and resignation struck me into helpless submission.

He left after a little while, and he never tried it again.

This was a terrible pattern with the men in my life. Why didn't I fight back physically or verbally? Why couldn't I protect myself? Especially against Carl, who was fine with taking abuse? I don't know. Maybe I was tired of fighting all the time. Maybe I deserved everything that happened to me.

I never asked Ava if he'd touched her, maybe because somehow I feel I knew the answer—I just couldn't bear to hear her say it.

When it was finally decided that we were moving, I couldn't have been happier. I hated that house Dad kept me trapped in. I hated the slather of bitter memories coating the place, the rusted burners that cooked the same bland food over and over. I hated the stench, which I never did get used to. Each moment in there was a renewal of bygone adversities. Even the buried memories couldn't sleep for long. Now I would finally be in a home I'd known my whole life: my grandparents' house. Back to betterness. A tabula rasa in the middle of a hurricane.

Now Dad could relinquish even more of the responsibility that came with maintaining a home. Not that he was going out of his way to make it easier for us. The shortcuts he took were solely for himself. He was rather skilled at conning and contriving if he knew he could be successful at it.

"I'm raising four kids on my own, their mom tried killing them," he sobbed into the phone. "Please cut me a break."

Then he didn't have to pay his electric bill. He wasn't lying about what happened, at least. But those were crocodile tears. A weird pity arose for me hearing my dad bullshit so blatantly. He was so desperate he was willing to pretend to actually care about us.

"Please," he begged the Dominos delivery man. "I'm just a single dad."

Free pizza. Which he and Matthew ate in wolfing bites in front of us.

When my grandparents eventually decided to move to Illinois, it hurt. But at least it gave us a chance to live in a nice home for a while and go to a good school district. The house was big enough that I could avoid Dad if I needed to—plus the furniture and all the towels smelled like Grandma and Grandpa. The dynamic shift was finally in my favor. The arid landscape had turned at last. For once my reality aligned with my wishes. There was even a big white washing machine and dryer, and I intended to use it whenever I wanted. Then the other kids wouldn't be repulsed by me at school. Things could finally be different for me. I could be a somebody. Someone worthy of love and adoration. It felt like a fresh start—but dad and Matthew quickly snuffed out my hope.

Grandma had a beautiful garden in the backyard—Dad walked out in the dark one night, totally blitzed, and pulled up every plant. He smoked in the house so that the Grandma and Grandpa smell quickly went away. He stained the beautiful white carpet with engine grease and beer. Matthew, eager to mirror his dad, threw a pumpkin through the front window, knocked down the picket fence, and filled the living room and kitchen with garbage.

As usual, there was nothing I could do but watch. I tried not to cry as I wondered where we would go next. Slowly the romantic rendering of our lives disintegrated into ephemera, back to where it came from. Born from an illusion. Another chance for life to be systematically dismantled by the ones who were supposed to love us.

When Grandma and Grandpa eventually served him an eviction notice, he waved the letter in the air. "See kids? They don't care about you. Come here, Mattie."

That's when he and Matthew used sledgehammers to destroy the water main line. Two angry, gruff entities unleashing their hatred upon something beautiful. I think Dad disdained beautiful things because beauty was unattainable for him, an opposite reflection in the wake of his endless destruction. He never could endure the careful time that beauty requires. He was never smart enough, never patient or observing enough. Plundering was so much easier, a quick corroboration of manhood.

The extent of the damage made my heart ache. I tried to clean up the wet basement and ruined décor, but it was hopeless. The delicate structure that had been upholding our lives for the past few months floated limp and drowned around me. All those meticulous hours of creation instantly obliterated. The home had become another ruined house—anything Dad touched was sucked dry of its joy. Every possible advent to life ended up in ruin. Every joyful experience mutilated to mockery.

They cost my grandparents $20,000 in repairs. I wondered if it was worth it to them. If I was worth that amount of money—worth anything.

Whenever Dad went to the bar, he came home with a woman. I hated all of them, but none more than Shannon.

With bright red hair and crooked teeth, Shannon stayed far too long. Days and then weeks. She immediately tried to be a "mother to us," which made me sick. She tried to ask me about school and boys. She wanted to play with Ava and Elijah and help with their homework. How dumb did she think I was anyway—how desperate? I'd been mothering both myself and the twins for this long. I wasn't interested in the newest flavor of the week trying to coddle me and dig into my psyche. It all seemed disingenuous, suspicious. Abuse was the default, not this emotional posturing. Besides, if she was with my father, how good could she really be?

I walked into the kitchen one day and found her braiding Ava's hair.

"What are you doing?" I demanded. I was enraged by this scene, more than I should have been. But the sight of her faux-motherly hands trying to gentrify my sister set a terrible ringing inside of me. We didn't need a mother. Who was this presumptuous stranger that felt entitled to this position, just for sleeping with my sleazy father?

"Braiding—"

"Get your hands off her!" I sprang forward and shoved her.

"Bob!" she shrieked, disappearing down the hall, suddenly cutt off of her nurturing inclinations. She knew this sort of thing warranted a beating.

"Hey," Ava said sadly, her hair half-braided and falling in her face.

"Shut up, Shamu." This made her bow her head in shame, her shag-head falling in disparate pieces over her face.

"Miss Jenson says you shouldn't make fun—"

"Zip it, Free Willy."

The way I treated my sister during this time is one of my deepest regrets. All I wanted was a role model, yet I wouldn't be one for her—refused to be. How could I model myself after something nonexistent to me? What paragon did I have to emulate? The idea of forging my own image of actualization was far too painful for me to even entertain. My vision expanded no further than surviving from day to day. There was no such thing as foresight in a lifestyle spent waiting for scraps.

Shannon sulked off to her room, and Ava to hers.

The sudden silence stunned me. It only took one expression of contempt to clear out all the life from the room. One thoughtless, fell swoop of rage. Maybe I was just as much of a monster as Dad.

I stood in my bedroom and tapped my foot, arms crossed. I could hear Dad's classic country through my door. I heard Matthew on the phone, shouting. Ava and Elijah played noisily. It was almost midnight. My muscles were tight—I had to get out of here.

I slipped out the back door unnoticed and walked across the yard to Dad's garage. I knew what I'd find there—a big silver Volkswagen with the key in the ignition. I was only 14, but I felt confident that I could drive it.

I turned the key, and the car rushed to life beneath me. I smiled—and off I went.

It wasn't so hard, I thought. I stopped at all the red lights and I used the blinker when I turned. I turned the radio up as loud as it went, feeling like a real classy woman. Worldly and seasoned, I could decide the whim of my instant fate: left or right, north or south, Texas or anywhere else. Independent at last.

In the Wendy's drive-through, I pulled away from the payment window and toward the pickup one. This freedom was delightful—I could just head out and grab a burger whenever I wanted. This is what it was like to be your own person. When I was 17, life would be different. I would be happy. I would go anywhere I desired, become anyone I wanted. No longer would I be tied to the humiliation of home life and its ridicule.

That's when the engine spluttered. I stepped on the gas, but it didn't do anything. And then silence. The dumb heat of failure flooded my face. Another possible fate of freedom instantly revoked. I tried not to cry as I fiddled with the ignition, cars honking behind me.

That night, I left that old car in the drive-through and walked all the way home in the dark. A few cars honked as they whizzed by, so I drew nearer to the dark. I didn't want to be seen by anybody, stewing in my impotent aftermath. At home, I woke Matthew up. My old compatriot. Maybe he'd understand. He was a veteran of failed hijinks.

"Hey, I need help," I whispered. "Please."

But when I told him what happened, he laughed loudly. "Bob!" he called, sprinting out of the room. "This bitch wrecked a customer's car!"

The next day, Dad grounded me for a month. But he didn't hit me. Instead, he called all his friends and told them I jacked a car and left it on the highway. He failed to tell them it was his customer's car, probably out of embarrassment. I was just another one of his stunted offspring inadequate at living up to his level of champion criminality. "The dumbass," he laughed. Everyone else laughed, too.

At my new school, the teachers actually cared about the students. I wasn't used to this. It was at once refreshing and suspicious.

I don't know which teacher referred me, but someone found out my mom was in prison, and I was put into a mentorship program. A woman named Melissa Sampson was swiftly assigned to me—she was a doctor, and her husband was a pilot. I was amazed by her. She was the living fruition of all the *right* choices in life.

Every Wednesday Melissa brought me lunch and just, well, talked to me. It was the first time I had interactions with people who weren't broken. With her shiny brown hair and soft, clean sweaters, she seemed like an angel to me. She wore glasses and smiled a lot, even though she seemed tired around her eyes. She was a busy woman, after all, and she worried about a lot of things. I mean, if she cared so much about me, a total stranger, I couldn't imagine how much emotional energy she expended on her patients, her husband, her children. She was the prototype of a mother I could only wonder about.

She seemed from another planet, always bearing new wisdoms. She brought me foods I'd never even heard of.

"What is this?" I asked, unwrapping the foil. It smelled incredible, even better than Taco Bell.

"A burrito—it's from Chipotle!"

"From what?"

Melissa bit into her burrito, smiling. "I thought kids loved

Chipotle."

I babysat for Melissa's kids often—a girl and twin boys. I imagined they were the double of me and the twins—the paradigm of the life we could have lived under an entirely different auspice. She let me spend the night frequently—though she didn't say so, I knew it was because she didn't want me around Dad. I relished in the clean sheets and towels there, the pleasant conversation. The children were so well-behaved and agreeable. There was never any tension in the air, no pretense of sudden fights or drunken monologues.

The environment at Melissa's reminded me of Aunt Renee' house—church every Sunday and Wednesday, age appropriate shows and movies, full parental involvement. Each day I witnessed these manifestations of a healthy family unit. Something in me remained wary, guarded, but my trust in her was never broken. The vicissitudes that accosted me in daily life were nonexistent here. The family brought me along on their trips, bought me presents, and generally cared about me.

It was bizarre. The whole era seemed to me like some fragile dream, one wrong turn away from the usual terror of lucidity.

CHAPTER 13

I was grateful to have Melissa, but there was only one person who made life truly worthwhile for me: Beau. I could write an entire book about him. Maybe I will. Naturally, there are no adequate words to assign to him. It's simply a feeling.

When I first spotted Beau in sixth grade, I thought he was gorgeous. He was a wrestler, stocky and strong. Despite his popularity, he was never mean. He was the embodiment of the type of male I'd never known—kind and caring. He would be my first real crush, and the love of my life.

He and Matthew were close friends, and Beau came around the house often. I'd make sure to do my hair and makeup whenever I saw his truck pull up. I became a regular Pavlov puppy at the sound of his tires, rushing to my mirror to make myself look like the girls in the magazines. Desirable. Maybe even slightly mysterious, if I could get my eyeliner right.

"Hi Beau," I'd say in my sweetest voice when he came in, slouching against the doorway for coolness.

"Oh, hey Emma."

I was just amazed he knew my name. Matthew always hurried him away, but sometimes I'd catch him smiling at me, or lingering by my bedroom door when he didn't have to. A silent exchange existed between us—a sideways glance or a smile that could set me straight for weeks. All I'd have to do was imagine him looking my way to drag me out of my depressions. He was my beacon of light beneath the perpetual awning of home life.

Beau's life wasn't bad, but his parents were hard on him. They'd both been wrestlers and wanted their kids to be star athletes. Beau was the star quarterback. He would make the front page of the newspapers. He was either admired or envied, and treated them all just the same. There was some deep oasis of assurance within him, a source that drew me to him. A gentleness.

Before long, Beau became my protector. He kept me safe from Dad and Matthew every time they tried to hurt me, always stepping between us. He became the buffer between me and the daily violence, a link to a better life. Eventually they were too scared of Beau to try anything with me anymore. The tumultuous shoreline was beginning to recede, the harbor steadying.

For the first time in a long time, I was safe.

I assumed Beau would want a pretty Barbie girl, and I was wearing my brother's clothes to school. I tried my best to incorporate Laura's advice into my daily beauty routine, but it usually didn't turn out how I envisioned. The mirror never produced a portrait I was proud of. But he liked me.

One day I was on Myspace, scrolling aimlessly, when I received a message from him: *Hey, I was wondering if you wanted to go on a date?*

It was December 6, 2006—I know, because I have a tattoo commemorating the date. It was one of the happiest days of my life.

Beau's parents didn't want him around me—I was a distraction. He worked out less and dropped football because of me. I never asked him to do any of this, but it was clear that I required a certain level of attention to feel secure. They hated me for this, but that was fine—I was used to being hated. Being hated by proxy was especially easy.

I quickly became alpha. I was around mean men all the time, and I'd learned not to be pushed around. Especially after what happened with Carl. I promised myself never to let something like that happen to me again, to never indulge that lowest level of powerlessness. What I said went with Beau—he was willing to do what I wanted when I wanted, no questions asked. It was a new feeling in my life, one of the positive byproducts of being a doormat for so many years. I was beginning, at last, to become my own person, to find a space to fill outside of the wasted icon of my mother.

He wasn't book smart. I did all his homework for him, but I didn't mind. His tenderness toward me compensated for the time I spent on it. He would send it to me along with little love letters through our friend Devin. For once I felt the warm symbiosis of a healthy relationship, the symptoms of being loved for my raw self. Colleges wouldn't take Beau because of his GPA, so he had one crappy job after another —Big Lots, Walmart, cleaning carpets. This never bothered me. He was way more involved and disciplined than my father had ever been, and that alone was astounding to me.

I was sitting in the passenger seat of his truck looking out at the stars when he turned to me, looking nervous. He had the habit of biting the inside of his cheeks when he was sad. For a moment, my stomach dropped.

"My parents are kicking me out," he sighed.

"Seriously? Fucking assholes," I said.

"Well. I was thinking I could stay with you." He looked toward me with wide heavy eyes. Offered a slow, ginger smile.

Something lit up inside me. I couldn't imagine anything I'd like more—except maybe having a place of our very own. But I knew that time would come. Once again the nebulous future opened to me, the way it had but few times before. I looked to him, tawny streetlamps briefly possessing his face and retreating back into shadow. The faint flickering of my future.

"EMMA!" Dad's voice boomed down the hall. I sat up in my bed, heart racing. Ready to defend myself, for the rushing rote of abuse. Beau stood up and moved toward the door.

"Emma, are you fucking kidding me?" Dad screamed as he burst into the room. "A fucking condom coming up in the toilet right now?"

I felt my face go red—I didn't know you couldn't flush a condom down the toilet.

"Easy," Beau warned, stepping in front of me. His figure loomed well over Dad's, who was permanently hunched against a wall or doorway.

"You piece of shit." Dad lunged forward in sloppy steps, but Beau held him back easily. Beau was young and fit, and

Dad was an old alcoholic. He stumbled like a limp goose on the other end of Beau's arm, swinging loose shots with fists sticky with beer. There was great satisfaction in seeing the immediate failure of his efforts, all his concentrated rage boiling away to nothing.

It was one of the last times Dad would try to hurt me.

I expected Beau to be loyal to me at all times, yet I couldn't return the gesture. I simply acted on any feelings I had in a given moment. I didn't take the time to think things through—I just did what I wanted and asked for forgiveness later. Nevertheless, I was sure Beau and I were going to get married. I loved him so much.

And he would always forgive me.

When Beau introduced me to wrestling, it quickly became my outlet. My coach had a pretty good idea of what was going on at my house—all the teachers and administrators at the school seemed to. Pinning people to the floor using headlocks and half-nelsons seemed like the natural sublimation for my situation, one that required methodic discipline and afforded respect.

"Here," Coach said gruffly, extending his arm toward me after practice.

"What is it?" I panted, wiping the sweat from my forehead.

"Here." He shook the card in his hand. "Just take it."

It was a Walmart gift card.

"Buy a sports bra and sliders," he said, already turning

away. "Okay?"

This was the same coach who made fake flyers stating we'd be gone for the weekend because of a wrestling event. He just wanted to give me a break from Dad. Being surrounded by a network of people who knew the ugly details of my life was both a source of shame and relief. I didn't have to struggle so much anymore to disguise all those festering truths—not that I was very successful at it in the first place.

"Okay," I said, something funny tugging at my heart. "Thanks Coach."

I did buy a sports bra and sliders—but I only got to wear them a few more times after this, because soon I tore my hamstring badly.

Dad refused to take me to the doctor, so I just lay in bed and suffered. The pain seared all along the right side of my body, sometimes incapacitating. I felt the tender sickness of a newborn. Matthew only saw this as a perfect opportunity to attack me. He came into my room in the middle of the night and yanked me from my bed.

"Hey," I mumbled, shaken roughly from my sleep. Pain shot through my leg like lightning as Matthew shoved me to the floor. As my eyes adjusted, I saw him grab a snow globe from my dresser. He cocked his arm back and aimed it at me.

What he didn't know was that Beau was watching from my closet, where he'd retreated to when he heard him coming. He burst out and punched Matthew in the face, busting his chin open. He staggered back, holding his bleeding face.

"What the fuck?" Matthew demanded. He kicked me in the side and ran from the room. "Bob! Bob!" Droplets of blood singed sideways through the air after him.

"Thank you," I whispered to Beau, holding his face in my hands. I swept my fingers along his stubble, the rugged shield of safety. A man to be close to. He planted a kiss on my mouth and ducked swiftly out the window.

"Cops are coming, Emma!" Matthew shouted from the kitchen. I struggled to my feet and back into bed. Despite the revived agony of the injury, a solace bloomed through me.

I didn't care if the cops came. They'd come many times before. Nothing much ever came of it, a glitchy scene I had re-watched to a tiresome memory.

This time, though, they actually seemed to listen to me. This time they believed me. I don't know why. Maybe it was easier to feel sorry for me when I was an invalid. Someone who clearly couldn't fend for herself.

I watched from my bedroom window as Matthew was chauffeured into the back of the cruiser, blood running down his shirt. The tired platitude of family history repeated itself, a cheap Blockbuster film. He wore the same blank expression of Tim after his foiled plan to drown us. He stared at me dimly from behind the window, like a fortune teller trapped in a crystal globe. He was arrested for family violence. He had to get stitches and spend the night in jail. It was one small consequence after years of violence and assault. One small blip in his treacherous track record. I like to imagine that he was crying in that cell, scared that someone might hurt him if he closed his eyes. I wanted him to feel as fearful and pathetic as he made me feel, to steal his wicked joy from him and test it out for myself.

"Piece of shit whore," Dad sobbed, his eyes red. "You're such a fucking bitch, Emma. Goddamn." He desperately chugged the rest of his beer and threw it on the floor, hanging his head. Slobber drooled out from his lips, dripped onto his boots.

I simply smiled.

I had to find Beau and tell him how much I loved him.

CHAPTER 14

Christmas wasn't what it used to be. Dad's empty, filthy house just made me miss Mom's decorations. All the crazy lengths she went to make it special. The only thing that came close to holiday lighting was the buzzy fluorescent light reflecting from the chorus of half-crushed beer cans. Dad disdained Christmas music and the sentimental concept of "family bonding."

"Emma." Dad shoved a $100 bill at me. "Get the twins presents."

As usual, I wandered around Walmart picking presents out for Ava and Elijah. Elijah always got more, because he was into cars and they were less than $1. Contriving femininity through glitter and pink plastic was apparently quite an expensive endeavor, but I tried my best to pick out things that would dazzle Ava enough to distract from the disparity. She would only get a couple of presents, and she would sit and cry as she watched Elijah open all his. Dad didn't care—he hated Ava the most. She stood no chance, being a girl and resolutely *not* his daughter.

I watched her cry, her cheeks pink and shining. I watched Dad chuckle from the kitchen table, beer in hand. Deep down I knew it wasn't, but it somehow felt like all my fault. I struggled against the competing roles of compliant daughter and protective sister. So far, they seemed mutually exclusive. Our small pool of joy was a scarce resource. It couldn't be had by all at once, and it had its favorites.

I stood over the sink scrubbing dishes, and Matthew tapped my shoulder.

"Hey, I think we need to get out of here," he said urgently, his face serious.

My hands were hot and itchy from the soap. I recoiled—he was standing way too close to me. He smelled too much like Dad now. We all did. "Huh?"

"Bob is a terrible person. We need to run away." His expression was oddly stoic, as if he'd been masticating on this epiphany for a while. It was impossible to gauge his level of sincerity.

I paused and turned toward him. "Really?" At any moment, I thought he'd break into laughter and do something to me, rat me out just for the brutal entertainment of the backlash.

I'd always wanted to run away. But he always sided with Dad, and I was too scared to go alone. Even if I had to endure Matthew's abuse in a foreign place, it was better than the tumultuous cycle of abuse at Dad's house. I trusted that some feeble thread of companionship still existed between us, the vague fact of familiarity that tied siblings together. There was nothing more commiserating than suffering beneath the same hegemonic force for years. Even if the suffering wasn't equal.

"Yeah. Go pack your shit."

But I didn't have any shit. I just put my cellphone in my pocket and laced up my shoes. Plus I was too anxious to formally pack. The need to exit the house before Dad found out rushed hysterically into my body, making me tremble. This was it. This was all it took. Just a couple of steps to freedom.

"I'm really glad you decided this," I said to him as we walked down the street. "He's such an ass. We don't need this shit anymore." It was late and breezy, but I felt fully awake. The pedestrian landscape began to resonate a strange newness. The real-life theater of liberation, step by step. I could feel a future coming toward me.

We made it to the other side of the neighborhood before Dad started blowing up Matthew's phone. The loud ringing shocked my body with panic. I plugged my ears to try to keep the sound out. I couldn't bear to let him ruin another advent, to take away all of my opportunities.

"Shit," he said. "He's pissed." He glowered at the phone, twisting his face up with tragedy as if Dad were standing right in front of us.

"Just ignore him," I said. "Please, let's just keep on going. He doesn't know where we are. Don't be an idiot."

We walked on for a few minutes. The phone kept regurgitating its awful noises, over and over again. I could imagine Dad on the other side, foaming beer and fury. Eyes bugged out and low, searching for a scapegoat to sacrifice. Then Matthew shook his head, slowed his pace. "I think we'd better go back." He turned the other way.

Reluctantly, I followed him home, back to the trail of tears we came from.

"You little fuckers," Dad shouted when we came in. "Where do you think you're gonna go? Huh?" He stood up from his favorite chair, lumbering toward us with a cigarette in his mouth. Beer cans shot out from beneath the unstable coordinates of his heavy boots.

"Emma wanted to go," Matthew said casually.

I sat down in the kitchen, put my head in my hands. Was I ever going to break this impervious loop? How to be free from this terrible karma I was enlisted to? I felt spineless and exhausted, felt the gravity of their eyes cruising over me. I sighed, trying not to crack into tears.

"Shocking," Dad muttered, laughing gruffly in his usual sadistic way.

I closed my eyes and thought of Beau. He was my only hope now for a better life, my only window out.

"She said you're an ass," Matthew added, leaving the room with a shrug.

Dad grabbed my hair and yanked me to the floor, thumping my skull against the tile with gleeful swings. Beyond the intermittent bashing, I could hear his laughter.

I was a cashier at Walmart, but I didn't have a car. I was leaving 45 minutes before my shift started to walk there and clock in on time. It was an extra stressor that made me swiftly develop my sense of timing: making sure the twins were fed before I left, tidying the house so Dad wouldn't scream at me when I came back, finishing homework for Beau, all before venturing out into the weather to work for eight-plus hours.

Eventually Dad bought me a car. God knows why—maybe he was simply working on a plan to take it away from me. Anything to cause me some pain. At any rate, I knew it was just another symptom of his unknowable complexes, the dark-matter logic of his mind. I wasn't convinced of its reality, of his reasons, so the car remained to me some transient fantasy.

It was a 1988 Oldsmobile Delta in red—the longest, ugliest thing on this earth. It had actual carpet on the inside, stained with the dank scent of cigarettes. It had a loud, tinny engine that drew disdainful looks from other drivers. I would park as far away as possible from my destination so nobody would mentally attach me to that 'boat'. Still, I was grateful I didn't have to walk anymore. Now I wouldn't have to worry about showing up to work soaked as a shower curtain every time it rained.

"Say," grinned Scott, our neighbor and Dad's friend. "You oughtta let me take that baby for a spin." He ran his finger along my car as I was getting ready to leave for work. I never liked Scott—he was of the same ilk of every other man I'd encountered in my life. Greasy, dirty, crude.

"Sure, you can take her!" Dad said. "She's a nice one, ain't she?"

"Sorry, I'll be late for work," I said quickly, trying to move past. The two of them bent over the hood leering at it as if it were a woman.

"I bought the car," Dad snapped, thumping his fist on the roof. "Scott wants to drive it. He'll take you to work."

"Don't worry baby," Scott winked at me, placing a hand on my back. He smelled of sour liquor. I felt his rankness leaking off onto me and stepped back.

"I have to get going," I insisted, trying to shoulder my way into the driver's seat.

Dad reached out and snatched the keys from my hand, cutting my hand. A limp scribble of blood flooded my palm. He placed them in Scott's hand. One greasy palm to another, the dissolute link from degenerate to degenerate.

"Alright! Let's go, baby." Scott said with a wicked grin, thrusting the door wide open like a new prize. What business did he have helping himself to other people's things? What bizarre sense of ownership? Men like him astounded me with their infinite ways to pillage and commandeer.

I sat as close as possible to the door during the drive. But he still put his hand on my knee, squeezing it every so often and smiling at me. My skin crawled—I only had to make it a couple of miles. I could do this. I had become good at ceaselessly enduring the grim series of life's events. Though this was quaint compared to what I'd been through, a deep rage ignited inside of me; a festering flame. Another ugly, depraved man who felt entitled to my life, my things, my body.

"Here we are, sweetheart," he said as we reached the parking lot, stretching his arm over my headrest to turn toward me.

"You're fucking disgusting," I snapped as I got out of the car. "I'm never going to sleep with you, got it?" I slammed the door in his face as hard as I could and stomped off without waiting for a response. Anger scuttled around my ribs, pure and fermenting, the blood-warm heat of hatred.

If I'd told Beau, he would have literally tried to kill Scott. I was good at keeping dirty secrets like this. It was what my world started to revolve around. I was consumed with these unspeakable truths and scandals, in waking life and sleeping life and all those bleary in-betweens. The dull gut of guilt spun like a low fruit inside of me, constructed a narrow tunnel between me and reality. My world seemed soaked over with my own worst shames at every moment. Even the sporadic pockets of happiness were sullied.

Dad sold the Oldsmobile a couple of weeks later. I was unfazed. In fact, it was almost a relief that it was gone. Now I wouldn't have to worry about when or if he was going to get rid of it. It was simply gone. The now-empty cavity in the driveway looked like some sick joke, but I felt nothing.

When we got kicked out of Grandma and Grandpa's place in 2008, we had moved into a foreclosed house with a big filthy pool in the backyard. The lawn was overgrown with dying weeds and various forms of plastic. It looked symbolic. Shingles moldered, siding chunked off from years of asymmetrical rot. Crumbling cement stairs I could grind to dust with a few kicks. A good place to die.

"I'm just glad you're moving in with us," I said to Beau as we moved his boxes from the pickup into the house. "I don't know what I'd do if you weren't."

He took a large box from my arms and stacked it onto a pile in the front room. "What," he grinned, "you think I'd leave you here alone?"

Dimples pressed into his cheeks, and my heart melted. The way he looked at me was a confirmation of everything I'd ever wondered about. What else could I possibly want for as long as he was beside me? He was the first proof for me that I didn't require an entirely new life in order to better the one I already had.

That night, Dad stayed at his girlfriend Beverly's place and left all us kids alone in the new house. The windows weren't well insulated, so it was chilly and inundated with the sounds of car horns and passing miscreants. It felt like we were trying to make a home out of the naked bones of a stranger's abandoned history. It was a difficult task to do without much material inspiration—only my threadbare clothes and Dad's girlie portraits. Beau and I were unpacking boxes when I heard a thump from across the house.

"What was that?" I dropped the box from my grip and listened closely.

He straightened up, eyes on the door. "I don't know."

I heard a window sliding open.

"I think someone's coming in," I whispered, panic rising. I looked around for any potential weapons, but wasn't convinced of the clothes hanger's ability to fend off some meth-high psychotic.

Beau quickly stood and left my room. He had his fists all balled up the way he always did when getting ready to kick someone's ass. I listened to his footsteps move toward the back of the house. I wondered faintly if I should follow him down there just in case, but was reminded by my pulsating fear that he was perfectly capable of breaking a few bones on his own. *Hey,* I heard him say. *Get the fuck out of here!*

I sat on my floor and held my breath, heart blitzing like a maniac. Footsteps shuffled and then ran, and then it was quiet. I kept still to make sure the silence wasn't a farce. A surprise attack was always a possibility.

"Beau?" I whispered as footsteps shuffled closer to my door.

"They're gone," he said, stepping back into my room. He sat beside me and wrapped an arm around my shoulders. "Don't worry." I put my head on his shoulder, trying to understand his strength, to absorb some of his calmness. Years and years of imagining a man like this in the apses of my loneliness. Now I could feel him breathing beside me. My chest felt like a magnet, heady with sorrow and relief and gratitude.

The next day, I told Dad someone had broken in. He simply shrugged. "Long as they didn't take nothin." He spent most of his nights at Beverly's after that.

Magazines were spread out on my bedroom floor, air-brushed smiles staring up at us.

"I'd like to get a nose job to look like this," Cecelia said, planting her finger on one of the faces. The face was flat and sleek and angular. It didn't matter that it was hollow and falsified. It was beautiful. Who didn't want to be beautiful?

Cecelia was my old friend from Peachtree City. It felt good to have her here with me, talking just like old times. By this point, even the pretense of normalcy was impractical and pointless. I wasn't even embarrassed by our living conditions. I was tired of waiting for some platonic idea of perfection to reassemble my entire life before I allowed myself any joy. I was finding that I could be happy even in this desolation, as long as it was populated by people who cared about me. She had always been kind to me, detached from the taboo bubble of poverty that sullied me in the eyes of all my other classmates.

"Or lip fillers," I said, pointing to a different photo. I imagined myself with that plump, pink mouth. Feminine and seductive. It just seemed the protocol to achieving that was impossible, so there was always a forlorn feeling of defeat assigned to this kind of posturing. What was the point of that empty wistfulness anyway, now that I had Beau?

Dad had taken the door off of my bedroom for no particular reason, so we could hear Matthew watching television in the living room. I tried not to listen. It was a fruitless effort, however, as he had only become fonder of making himself as noticeable as possible in every situation. He couldn't even watch MTV without having some crude, prolific monologue to cuss at the television, and whatever female friend I had over.

"Emma, you bitch," Dad said now, entering my room. "Did I fuckin' say you could have people over?" He looked like some phased-out snapshot, smoke of a freshly burnt cigarette frothing out from around him. I imagined having the delicious ability to slam a door right in his face, but even that small satisfaction was not in the cards.

I stood up, my blood hot. All I wanted was to hang out and talk to my friend. To have a few moments of space and privacy. To be myself. Just one night. Just one normal night. But even that rusty little token of notion just had to be clumsily revoked. My patience for him was thinning, his idiocy becoming more apparent every day. Just a bored, useless addict.

"Is this your fucking house? Oh no, it's *my* fucking hou—"

I ran at him, tackling him to the floor easily. By this time I was bold when it came to physical altercations. I was always ready to hit someone if I needed to. Especially when it came to Dad. Any opportunity he presented me with to kick his ass, I was going to take it. The years of unlimited anger within me deepened and renewed by the day, by every one of his antics. I punched him until his nose bled, though in that moment I felt I could have bashed his brains to some dumb, dyslexic alphabet.

"Uh, I'll get going!" Cecelia called, stepping over us as we scuffled in the doorway. My chest sank as she closed the door behind her. We had hardly got to talk about her new boyfriend. I was devastated. The fuckery of home life always found a way to destroy all regularity.

"Ugh!" I stood up and brushed my clothes off. "I hate you! You ruin everything for me!" I spit at him, but it unfortunately missed and landed in a clump beside his head.

He chuckled as he shuffled off toward the kitchen, shaking his head and wiping the blood from his nose. Despite my aggression toward him, I could never win inside of his reasoning. I was just a girl. Didn't matter if I made his nose bleed or knocked him to his ass. I was just a timid version of Matthew, but much less effective, much more pathetic. A bitch, a whore.

"Fuck you!" Anger sizzled under my skin. Rattled my eyeballs. I placed both hands on my dresser and pushed, tipping it onto the floor with a bang. The glass figurine from atop it shattered against the wall. This was the only way I knew to relieve the hurt I was feeling. The only immediate relief available to me. To channel the harsh devastation within me into the world outside me, to make equal the chaos. To make visceral my lifelong pain.

I plucked my shoes from the floor and hurled them one by one against the wall. *Thud. Thud. Thud.* I couldn't throw them hard enough. The immeasurable destruction within me was satisfied with nothing less but obvious plundering. Everything within my line of sight felt irksome until brutally destroyed.

Through the gaping hole where my bedroom door should have been, I heard Dad laughing.

The last time I saw Aunt Renee alive, I met her and William at an Applebee's with Beau. She was perpetually surrounded by the scent of warm food, no matter where we were. The mark of a true mother. As we ate mozzarella sticks late at night, she smiled at me warmly.

"I'm so happy you two found each other. I love you kids." Her eyes were heavy with emotion. She was the only one who ever looked to me like that, like a Mom looks to her daughter. I felt grounded around her, and loved from all angles with Beau beside me.

Under the table, I squeezed his hand. "We love you too, Aunt Renee."

She was a rock throughout my life. She loved us more than our own parents. She was one of the scarce sources of health and affection, whose very presence on this planet made me feel better even when I was not with her. She was the one who first taught me that I was perfectly deserving of love. When she died, I shut down even further. It was more than just another loss. The love she had channeled to me since the day I was born had suddenly sparked shut forever. No more peanut butter sandwiches and sweet conversations, no more tender touches and words of wisdom. Sometimes it felt like I was living life from underneath a dark, heavy blanket. A volatile, nightmarish sleep.

I watched from the window above the kitchen sink as Matthew and four friends sat around the backyard. They smoked cigarettes and drank beer. They passed around a joint. Day by day fulfilling the empty, pitiful portrait of our father. Perpetually influenced by one substance or another. All the usual.

"Joey," I heard Matthew say seriously, and the other two stood and began to move around Joey as if it was their cue. My heart sank. I knew what this was. I'd seen it before. They were going to jump him. "I know you've been talking to Valerie."

"Huh? So what?"

Matthew spat at Joey's shoes as he moved closer. "So that's gonna get you fucked up." His jaw was jutted out and squared, fists falling into formation by his side.

Joey's eyes went wide with fear.

I ran out the back door and stepped in front of Matthew. “Come on, don't,” I said. I didn't want to see any blood today. I didn't want the cops to come again. By this time the officers were always aloof toward us, pestered. They were bored by the same strain of violence that found itself a home in our family, again and again. It was embarrassing to witness those geared-up policemen sighing, making strained eye contact with each other as if we were a bunch of low-class cretins.

“Fuck off, Emma.” Matthew pushed me, but I bounced right back. I knew he wanted to kill Joey. Someone had to do something. At least my violence was bound to some sort of moral compass. I couldn't let myself stand by while hearing the animal cries of another human. Especially not by the hands of someone so reprehensible as Matthew.

“Hey bitch!”

I turned to one of his other friends, Kevin. He was lifting his shirt to show me a gun in the waist of his jeans. Billy did the same. But I'd seen guns. I'd been threatened. Those were just some blasé icons to me, the mark of insecure boys posing as men. It infuriated me, the notion that I better watch myself, be a good bitch around the bad boys. I planted my feet firmly, more determined now than before, meeting their cold eyes as boldly as I could.

“Alright, fine,” Kevin sighed after several seconds of no one moving. “Matt and Joey just fight. One on one.”

“Fine,” Matthew snapped, taking off his shirt as if that would somehow give him better leverage.

Joey stood, and I smiled. He was much larger than my brother. I'd been dying for the opportunity to see him humiliated. It had been a while, and I had been humiliated plenty by him in the meantime. There was just no way to find justice for myself as long as we were living under the same roof as Dad. Except maybe vicariously through people he tried to jump. Joey moved quickly toward him with one heavy lunge. The fight was short, ending with a scream from Matthew. And a leaky pool of blood gushing from his nose and mouth.

I drove him to the ER, smug and victorious, and told him all the reasons why he was an asshole while he groaned over his various injuries. They yanked his shoulder back into its socket, which extracted a sound from him I'd never heard before. It made me giggle. That night, when he was passed out on pain medication, the twins and I drew penises on his face and arms in permanent marker—one of the strongest bonding experiences we'd ever shared.

Dad also found himself in his fair share of physical altercations—that's certainly where Matthew got it from. He had the most bizarre relationship with our neighbor Shaun; when they drank together, he called Dad white trash, and Dad called him a racist word that I could never see myself saying. They laughed like it was the funniest thing in the world.

One night, Dad and Shaun were sitting in the garage drinking with Shaun's teenage son, Dustin. Matthew and I were standing around as well, nothing else to do, listening to them exchange irreverent claims.

"You couldn't sack a broad if you were the last cracker in

town," Shaun laughed, leaning back in his lawn chair.

Dad shook his head. "And you couldn't if you were the last monkey on Earth!"

Dustin stood up; he was at least six feet tall and 200 pounds. "What the fuck did you just call my dad?" His obtuse figure made Dad look like some skeleton.

"Oh relax, son. Me and your daddy have a deal," he said, looking up toward him with passive amusement.

"It's not a deal I care for," he said, stepping toward him. He reached out and shoved Dad, toppling him over in his chair. His beer spilled over, streaking across the concrete. Matthew immediately stood and ran into the house to avoid further mutilation by guys obviously physically superior to him.

"Just sit down," I said, stepping between them.

"You sit down, little girl." He moved closer to me, trying to push me back. His boxy figure was like an irksome affront. Suddenly I felt like I had something to prove.

"Back the fuck up," I snapped.

"I will fuck you up, little girl—"

"Leave her alone, Dustin," Shaun said, but not with much conviction. They were clearly already a few beers in, lofty and fuzzed-up.

"Hey!" Our other neighbor Hector came running toward us. "What's going on?"

I reached out and shoved Dustin as hard as I could, and he

shoved back.

"Hey!" Hector pried us apart and held me back. I glared at Dustin to let him know I'd come back for him if I needed to. He looked like he got the message. I guess he wasn't expecting a girl half his size to assert herself so blatantly. What did he expect? He knew whose daughter I was.

Dad and Matthew beat up on me for years, yet I continued to protect them. They would never have done the same for me. In fact, not long after, Dad called the cops on me, claiming I was being aggressive—though I hadn't left my bedroom all day. When the cops showed up, they didn't even ask questions. They immediately put me in handcuffs. A familiar anger rose in me, hot and prickly. I felt the panic of the imagery I was fulfilling, the inevitability of it.

"Let me go!" I screamed, kicking and thrashing as I was dragged to the cruiser. Why did these people, who were supposed to serve and protect the public, take some bitter drunk's word for truth? Hadn't they seen me time and time again, at the opposite end of this very abuse I was being accused of? Inside, I kicked the back of the seats furiously. "I fucking hate you, Bob! You're not my fucking father!" I shrieked at the top of my lungs, straining my wrists against the cuffs.

Finally, the officer yanked me out of the car and sat me down on the road. "You need to calm down, ma'am. Calm down." She removed the cuffs. "Okay?"

I wiped the tears and sweat from my face. "Okay."

"Good. Now just behave."

She got in the cruiser and drove off, leaving me sitting in the middle of the road, crashing from the emotional surge. My entire body was awash in hysterical undulation—of grief and anger and confusion and accusation. I thrashed among these virulent states until I felt like throwing up, until all my energy was expended out onto the road around me. I stayed there until it got dark, glittering with broken glass and nighttime. I stayed there until I felt the electricity of this defeat drain completely.

When I finally decided to go back inside, I could hear Matthew in his bedroom, beating his girlfriend Karen. It was a familiar sound—Matthew cursing. Karen crying. Muffled slaps and thuds. Every once in a while the shattering of something that got thrown or turned over.

I closed my eyes and took a deep breath. *Don't go in there. It's not your problem. It's not your problem. Stay out of it.*

I could feel my legs standing up. Walking toward Matthew's room. I saw my hands grab his shirt and pull him off Karen. An out of body experience ignited by the recursive devastation of violence. I couldn't help myself anymore. This was my body's natural reaction, a way for it to keep homeostasis with my mind. Which meant allowing less bullshit and abuse.

"Leave him alone," Karen cried, rushing to his side. Her face was wet and puffy. Perfectly dumb.

"Get the fuck out," Matthew said, shoving me out the door and slamming it on my face.

Moments later, the sounds of sex replaced the sounds of

fighting. It disgusted me that she would indulge that level of intimacy with someone like him. To lay in vacant complacency beneath a criminal.

"He's a child molester, Karen!" I screamed through the door. I'd told her many times that he had touched both me and Ava, hoping it would make her leave. But she didn't seem to care. She was desperate enough to assimilate all types of assault into her boyfriend's image without question. I hated her for this. I thought she was pathetic for allowing these things to happen to her without any protest.

The moment the clock hit midnight on my 17th birthday, I grabbed my backpack and ran the hell out of that house. Never again would I depend on anyone else to change my life. It took me this long to learn that I was the only one I could truly trust. The only one delirious enough to believe that the future was not yet done with me.

This was the night the world opened for me, cautiously and distantly, the swarthy mirage of freedom blooming dark and new beneath a moonless sky. The scent and scene of other people's lives moved dimly at the edge of my vision. Behind shuttered windows the same familiar scenes; the rote ritual of living and breeding and dying in poverty. All the landmarks of memory that accumulated in my life up until this point ripened in this final vow.

As I walked further from home, passing each moldering mailbox and sagging fence, something moved within me. Something aqueous and fluid as saltwater. Some expanse, undying and ubiquitous. The stream of hopeless belief I had tided all my life suddenly flooded me. I felt the torrent of my past, of all the things that had happened to me, drown in the deluge of the present moment. None of Dad's nor Mom's inebriated fits could keep me from walking away from all of this.

This was my debutante ball. Walking with ripped shorts and a heavy bag along a weedy road. This was emergence into a world not my own. All the pastoral suitors of the bus station destinations waited in silence for me. Tickets and terminals of experience yet to be terraformed. Somewhere in the retching darkness my parents presented souring histories with self-pity eyes and swimming minds. The burden of the daughter transferred out of their hands at last.

Soon, in a distant scene unknown to me, I would arrive, and just on time. Strangers would lift their gaze to incorporate me into their reality, if only for a moment. That was good enough for me, to stand stark and alone against my own selfhood. For once, I saw how that singular rite could never be taken from me. From anyone.

A rickety car blasting country music sputtered past like some smoking lone wolf. Its license plate hung half off, trembling with near-freedom. I stretched my arms up toward the sky, looking up to the titian humming of the street lamps soaking their dim colors into the great caul of blackness. In a few hours, there would be sun. When it rose, I would find it and follow. The search would happen slowly, darkly, with the solar instinct of a sunflower.

THE END

ABOUT THE AUTHOR

Chelsea Nicole is a graduate of American Military University. Prior to going to college, she served in the Army for 5 years and 5 months as an ammunition specialist. She completed basic training at Ft. Jackson and her AIT at Ft. Redstone Arsenal. Chelsea was stationed in South Korea for 1 year then served her remaining time at Ft. Hood. Cry, Little Girl is Chelsea's debut novel. This book started off as a way to journal through the trauma she experienced as a child. She now lives in Texas with her husband and two children.

Contact the author:

Email: chelseanicolewriter1@gmail.com

Instagram: Chelseanicolewriter

Made in the USA
Columbia, SC
14 January 2022

53728362R00083